G000069695

NO PICNIC FOR SAM

Roderick Shaw

First edition published in 2015 by Heddon Publishing.

Copyright © Roderick Shaw 2015, all rights reserved.
No part of this book may be reproduced, adapted, stored
in a retrieval system or transmitted by any means, electronic,
photocopying, or otherwise without prior permission of the
author.

ISBN 978-0-9932101-6-7

Cover artwork by Roderick Shaw.

This is a work of fiction. Names, characters,
businesses, places, events and incidents are either the
products of the author's imagination or used in a
fictitious manner. Any resemblance to actual persons,
living or dead, or actual events is purely coincidental.

Book design and layout by Katharine Smith, Heddon
Publishing.

www.heddonpublishing.com
www.facebook.com/heddonpublishing
@PublishHeddon

Dedicated to my uncle RSM John Hazlehurst, killed during the Battle of Caen, and his wife, Pat Hazlehurst, and to all those who made the ultimate sacrifice.

The main characters in *No Picnic for Sam* are very loosely based on my uncle, aunt, and my childhood friends. The rest is purely fictitious.

Chapter 1

A nightjar quartered the field, feeding on the wing. Bats, using the same moonlight, feasted on the terrestrial nightlife. Ghost-like, a barn owl patrolled the hedges, looking for larger prey.

Moonbeams were interrupted by the tangle of wind-blown trees casting moving patterns across the old house which had stood for so long it had become a part of the landscape, blending in naturally against the backdrop of the tall dark wood to its right.

In the main bedroom, Alan Tait lay in a half sleep, listening to the sounds of the night in the house he and his family had moved into earlier that day. He drew comfort from Donna's presence next to him; his wife was in the deep sleep that can come only from physical exertion.

That morning, Alan had stood on the steps of the house, waiting for the removal van to arrive. It was a lovely spring day with a clear blue pastel sky. He watched a pair of buzzards riding the thermals a thousand feet up, calling in piercing tones and revelling in the sheer joy of flight. That joy spread like the birds' wings to Alan. He felt a visceral wave of optimism; the day was perfect for a move and he was looking forward to settling in and getting to grips with the challenges of their new home.

His two children ran excitedly towards the house from their exploration of the garden.

"What yer doing, Dad?"

"Just waiting for our furniture to arrive."

The van duly turned up and two overalled men emerged, shaking hands with Alan. The one who Alan took to be the boss was a slight, weasel-like man. He was built like a racing whippet and was equipped with a high-pitched bark. The other was tall and stooped, with the pallor of Lazarus.

The boss climbed into the cab and reversed the van into the driveway, bringing it as near to the front door as possible, and then he and Lazarus pulled away the huge white sheets that had covered the furniture, removed a trolley, and wrestled with a massive sideboard. They manhandled this with the odd profanity quietly thrown in, as they struggled through the doorway and lowered the sideboard gently onto the tiled hallway floor.

Lazarus took a couple of blasts on his inhaler while the boss leaned against the doorjamb, contemplating their next move.

Donna came out of the kitchen, greeting the men, "Like a drink, boys?"

"That would be lovely, both with milk, no sugar," squeaked the boss, "we're sweet enough."

Lazarus cracked his face with a toothy grin at this puerile attempt at humour.

The two men worked hard, huffing and puffing, only stopping for brews or when Lazarus, gasping, took out his inhaler to revive his flagging lungs. Donna was in control, directing operations. Boxes were unpacked, items removed from newspaper and found new homes.

The Tait children, nine-year-old Billy and six-year-old Molly, ran amok with their Border Collie Spey adding to the mayhem. Alan had named Spey after that famous Scottish salmon river and had actually christened him in Spey water brought home in a lemonade bottle. Consequently, or coincidentally, the dog - like Alan - had a fascination with water, especially the fast-flowing type.

"Al, you'd better put these rods away," Donna

shouted, "they'll get broken down here."

Alan didn't like the shortened version of his name; he considered it an unwelcome Americanism. He also disliked terms like 'spag bol' and 'mayo' which he felt sure Donna only used in order to annoy him.

Although the two men looked physically incapable, they had finished the job that day. Alan thanked them and paid the boss, adding an extra fiver for a drink.

"Thanks very much!" Donna shouted through the kitchen window and Alan ran up the drive to open the gate. The van trundled off down the lane, trying to avoid the numerous potholes. Alan watched it go, noting the slogan across the back of the vehicle: *'Our experience is moving'.*

I like that, he thought, *clever!*

Now, as he lay between the cool cotton sheets next to Donna, Alan thought that it had all gone very well. He switched off the bedside light and watched shafts of moonlight intruding through gaps in the curtain, flickering across the bed cover and making patterns on the bedroom wall. He lay still, shut his eyes, and listened to the sounds of the night.

Gradually, he became aware of scratching sounds coming from the loft directly above his head. Squirrels, he thought, or it could be a mouse; just as long as it wasn't a rat. Donna was petrified of rats and she wasn't overly keen on mice, but she was fast asleep anyway, oblivious to any sound.

As he lay in the darkness, listening to the scuffling sounds overhead, Alan imagined he could hear unfamiliar breathing in the room, almost as if there was someone else there. He felt a slight fear envelop him. The house was old and no doubt had history. It definitely wasn't Donna he could hear. He held his breath and listened, relaxing as he realised it was nothing sinister; all he could hear alongside his wife's steady breath was his own shallow breathing.

The village clock struck eleven, or was it twelve? Alan snuggled up to Donna's back, putting his knees against hers, and he himself fell into a deep, secure sleep.

The first awakening in their new home was heralded by sunlight invading the room with shafts of brightness piercing the tiniest chinks in the curtains. Outside, it was breezy and magpies rifled the debris in the guttering in search of food while the dawn chorus was dominated by a large rookery in the wood and pigeons cooed messages down the chimney.

The front of the house was south-facing and enjoyed sunlight from dawn till dusk. The long gravelled drive was screened from the vegetable garden by rustic rose fencing. To the east, the tall wood acted as a windbreak, protecting the house from winds that blew across the open landscape. To the right of the drive was a large lawn that ran up to an ancient light, honey-coloured sandstone wall, against which grew two laterally-trained apple trees.

Alan stirred and opened one eye to the sunlight. Donna was still in the land of nod and he watched her lovingly, her blonde hair spilling across the pillow and a look of contentment on her face. She in turn began to stir and Alan used gentle movements, willing her to wake without her detecting his motive, but she was aware of his ploy as he had used it many times in the past. Sill he feigned sleep, closing his eyes and throwing in the occasional snore in the hope that Donna would get up first and make a cup of tea.

However, the charade came to nothing as the

bedroom door banged open and Spey raced in, jumping straight on top of Alan and smothering him in a frenzy of licking affection, imprinting paw marks and scratches on his chest.

"Get off! Bloody dog!"

"It's only because he loves you," interjected Donna.

"OK, I love him too, but he could be a bit more gentle," Alan complained, pointing at the scratch marks on his chest, "his bloody claws are sharp, look at these!"

"Don't be such a wimp, there's no blood is there?"

Two bed-ruffled children bundled in after the dog.

"Who let the dog up?" Alan demanded.

They replied in unison, each accusing the other. Donna by now was wide awake, admonishing the children, "You two, out! Go and comb your hair and put some clothes on!"

Billy replied, "But it's Sunday, Mum."

"Out!" she emphasised, with a resoluteness that had the desired effect. She then turned to Alan, "I'll get you a cuppa, darling, then the first job for you when you get up is to get the Aga going. Let's hope it lights."

On moving-in day they had used a double camping stove for tea-making and in the evening had a picnic, which Donna had prepared early that morning.

Alan sprawled out, stretching his legs and enjoying the freedom of the full width of the bed. He turned the bedside lamp on, picked up a page from an old newspaper that had been wrapped around the lamp, and read some two-week-old news. He stretched his right leg from under the duvet and, using his heel, opened the curtain wider. Bright light filled the room with optimism, prompting him to rise and open the other side.

Donna came in with a mug of tea, saying with some

surprise in her voice, "You up then?"

"Yes, what a super day." He put the tea on the windowsill and looked out across the field to the front of the house. There was a man some way off, standing amongst what looked like sugar beet. He was looking towards the house and at his side was a small terrier.

A fly landed on Alan's hand and in the time it took him to brush it off and pick up his tea, the man and the dog had disappeared. Alan scanned the field from foreground to background and from right to left but there was no sign of either of them. That seemed decidedly strange; there was no way they could have left the field in the time he had looked away. Alan opened the window and popped his head out so that he could see if there was any movement beyond the drive.

He could see a good way along from their bedroom window and the lane was empty as far as he could see. *Very odd,* he thought, *not a dicky bird*. He stood, thoughtfully sipping his tea and pondering what he had or hadn't seen. There was definitely someone there, very interested in the house. Had he been in some sort of uniform? Alan couldn't be sure and the early morning mist hadn't helped. He couldn't understand how the man and dog could have disappeared in a matter of seconds. Although there was a morning mist blanketing the ground, those figures had been real, he was sure of it.

Alan remained looking out across the field with a puzzled expression as he stroked the bristles on his chin. Picking up the duvet, he gave it a good shaking before laying it back on the bed, fluffing up the pillows, then, after one last puzzled glance at the field, he went to the bathroom.

This was the one room the last occupants had put in order. Alan took his time shaving before showering and dressing in old jeans and a grubby sweater. The smell of bacon rose from the kitchen, prompting him to accelerate. He pulled up his socks and put on his boots.

On top of the Aga, Donna had set up the camping stove and the meat sizzled away in the frying pan. The children were sitting at the massive table, eating beans and sausages.

"By 'eck, that smells a bit good," Alan said.

"It should be, it's home-cured from Maybury's Farm, there's no white gunk coming out of this," Donna enthused.

The children said excitedly, "Can we go out to play?"

"Only when you've eaten your breakfast," Alan replied.

"But Dad, I've had enough food, I dunner want to get fat," Billy argued.

"I want to see two clean plates, no ifs, or buts, it's as simple as that," Alan ordered resolutely.

Once the children had cleaned their plates Donna said, "You can go out now, but wash your hands and faces, and Billy - you put your jumper on the right way round... it's inside out as well... and both of you, stay in the garden."

Spey followed the children outside, jumping up and barking excitedly. Alan cracked three eggs and scrambled them, then loaded the toaster with two slices of bread.

He stood about a yard back. When the toaster popped, the toast flew out at speed, high into the air. You'd need to be a Gordon Banks to stop it hitting the deck.

"We'll have to get a new toaster," said Donna.

"No, no, no! It's unique, it's fun, it's a challenge."

Her fast response was, "I can't spare the time to play bloody goalies or whatever you call them with a toaster."

They sat down to breakfast, Donna saying, "I'll be glad when you've got the Aga going, I want to do some real cooking. I know it's only been a day, but I'm fed up with camping and I've always wanted an Aga, preferably one that works - and a pop-up toaster, not a missile launcher."

Alan quickly changed the subject, "I think the kids like it here, do you?"

"Yes, but your first job's still the Aga."

"Okay, I get the message."

Chapter 2

The kitchen door flew open. A red-faced Molly burst in, shouting, "Spey's playing with another dog up the end of the garden!"

"Where's he come from?" asked Donna.

"Dunno," said Billy.

"He's with the man," Molly added.

"What man?" Alan asked.

"The man, the man."

"Don't keep saying 'the man'," Alan said with some annoyance in his voice.

"There was a man in the field and I think it was his dog, a little dog," Molly said.

"There was no man!" Billy contradicted. "You know what she's like, always imagining things."

"There was too," his sister snapped back. "I hate you, Billy Tait. I did, I did, I seen him."

Donna interrupted, correcting her, "You didn't 'seen him', you *saw* him."

"Yes I did saw him, honest Mum."

"Well that's no excuse for you to use the hate word, especially to your brother."

"Well I did saw a man in the field, he looked like a soldier."

Molly's assertions tied in with Alan's earlier experience, but he said nothing. One thing he was dead certain of was that he had seen a man staring at their new home, and it had unsettled him somewhat, although it fascinated him rather than frightening him.

He left the children still arguing and went out to the coalbunker, filling up his scoop with smokeless fuel, taking it in and placing it by the Aga. Using a load of dry sticks and half a packet of firelighters, he waited till there was a good flame and poured on the solid fuel, a bit at a time. After a period testing the theory 'there's no smoke without fire', it gradually burst into life. Shortly, it filled the room with a warm glow.

That's worth a few Brownie points, thought Alan.

"Great," said Donna, "we can have a proper roast dinner tonight."

She loved roast beef and they had a nice piece of well-hung sirloin in the fridge. Donna also made a mean Yorkshire pudding.

On the Monday morning, Alan kissed Donna on the cheek, whispering, "See you tonight darling, do you want anything from town?"

"No, we've got leftover beef and all the trimmings for tonight, so we're fine, but don't be too late."

When he opened the front door to leave, he found a box full of new potatoes. He ran his thumb up one of them and the skin came off with ease. Donna was just coming downstairs so he held up the box. "Look at these lovely new spuds, freshly dug as well, they were on the doorstep."

"They could have been left there last night," she said. "We'll have a few of those with the beef as well, there's a bit of mint in the garden."

Finding mysterious gifts became a regular occurrence during the ensuing weeks; box after box of beautiful showcase vegetables were left on their doorstep but the benefactor never made themself known.

Meanwhile, the house renovation was coming along nicely. The dining room had been treated for damp, replastered, and Alan and Donna had painted it a cool off-white. With the table and chairs donated to them by an ageing aunt and new lightshades, it looked ideal for entertaining.

"Pity we've got no one to entertain," observed Donna.

"Well, Mum and Dad may come up for Christmas," Alan said, putting his arm around her.

The next room for renovation was to be the children's bedroom, which was in urgent need of attention. To take a look at the bulging ceiling from the other side, Alan decided to go up into the loft; he wanted to see if there was anything over the room and also to investigate any signs of animal activity which might be linked to the scratchy feet above his and Donna's bedroom.

On the landing, he put up the steps and climbed up. The ceiling was high and he could only just reach the cover to the loft. He pushed it off, stood on the very top step, and heaved himself up through the opening. The loft was long and had massive beams supporting the roof. Everything was covered with ages of thick dust and there were old dusty carpets and something unidentifiable at the far end. He shouted through the opening, "Is Billy there? Get him to bring up my torch, it's in the boot of the car."

Billy came up the stairs, triumphantly shouting, "I've got it Dad, do you want me to come up there?"

Alan dismissed this with a deflating, "No, just hand me the torch."

He shone the beam down to the far end where he could now see the object was a metal travel trunk with a name on the side. He could just about make out 'S. Left...', the rest of the name was partially hidden by a bit of old carpet.

He had no desire to scramble through the dust, as there seemed to be little else worth looking at up there and there were no immediate signs of animal activity other than a few woodworm holes that peppered the edges of the roof beams. This concerned him slightly, but the beams were so overspecified that the worms could nibble away for a hundred years with no risk to the roof.

Alan shone his torch at the trunk again. He estimated that it couldn't be far off the children's bedroom ceiling.

"Billy, can you hold the steps for me?" he shouted, "I'm coming down."

Alan got back through the opening and lowered himself gently, supporting himself on his elbows with his dangling feet searching for the security of the steps.

"Anything of interest up there, Al?" Donna called from the landing.

"No, just loads of space. No insulation apart from bits of old carpet, some newspapers, and there's a dip in the floor near to where the kids' bedroom is. Oh, and a big metal trunk and a water tank. Nowt much else. Oh yes, and there's no roof felt, they didn't use that in the old days."

"No wonder it's cold down here," Donna complained.

The following weekend, Alan was in the children's bedroom, pushing a broom against the pregnant bulge above his head. It moved and black dust drifted out where the wall joined the ceiling.

"What are you doing in there?" Donna asked.

"I'm just seeing how dodgy this ceiling is."

"Hang on," she said, "you don't have to be a construction worker to see it's dodgy. So leave it alone or you'll have the whole bloody lot down."

He stepped back sheepishly, feeling like a scolded schoolboy, leaning the broom against the wall. His destructive side wanted to bring the lot down, although he knew Donna was right.

The next day, they moved the children to the next room along the landing, moving everything out of the bedroom. Alan set to work sealing the door with polythene. Dressed in old clothes, a bobble hat, goggles and a scarf tied bandit-style around his mouth and nose, he pressed at the belly of the ceiling and leapt back as a huge lump of plaster and worm-eaten wooden laths hit the floor, followed by a huge black cloud of dust.

Donna shouted through the door, "Alan, are you alright in there?"

"Yeah! Don't come in, you were right - it didn't need much persuading."

He hooked the broom over the edge of the plaster and pulled, creating a thunderous bang when the large metal travel trunk came crashing through the ceiling to the floor, with more dust clouds choking the room.

"What the hell was that?" Donna shouted.

"It's a big travel trunk, scared the shit out of me."

After a good shift in the bedroom, he swept the debris into a pile. He then went along each beam with a clawhammer, removing any nails that remained. Then he found his attention turned to the metal trunk, which he could now see read 'S. Leftwich'. He lifted the clasp and opened the lid. Inside there was another small brown suitcase, a cricket stump and a *Daily Express*, brown with age, which showed Winston Churchill surrounded by cheering crowds.

'*Premier is to broadcast to the nation at 3pm. Two Days Holidays*', he read.

He dusted off the suitcase and put it by the door then took down the polythene, stripped and dropped his clothes in a pile and ran naked along the landing to the bathroom.

Black soot-like dust clogged his nostrils, coating his hands, eyes, face and hair. He turned the shower on hot and stood watching blackened water swirl and disappear down the plughole, reminding him of the shower scene in *Psycho*.

Hot-pink from the shower, with a towel wrapped around him, Alan went to the bedroom and put on fresh clothing. As he came down the stairs carrying the suitcase he had found in the trunk, a slim, athletic-looking tabby cat strolled into the hallway through the open front door. Spey chased in right behind it and the tabby immediately got height advantage by climbing the stairs. After a few initial skirmishes and lots of growling and spitting, both animals settled down, as if realising there was little point in fighting.

After this initial introduction, the cat soon became a regular visitor and then, after Donna started feeding him, he became the latest addition to the Tait family. Due to his peculiar trotting gait, Donna named him Trotsky, and the cat knew he had acquired a new comfortable home.

Back in the kitchen, Alan wiped the brown suitcase, removing ages of dust.

"Bugger," he said, "it's locked."

"Well we're not going to keep it, so force it open," said Donna. She too was curious to discover its contents. Alan forced a long screwdriver under the clasp and levered it and the lock off in one go. He opened the case expectantly but inside there was just an old well-worn cricket ball, a set of cricket bails, and an old photograph.

Donna picked up the picture and blew the dust from it. There were creases across it, a corner was missing, and it was brown, faded and cracked with age. The photograph was of a young pretty woman and a dog, sitting near a stream. She turned it over. On the back was written *'Mary and Patch, Great Mynd 1934'*.

"Let me see," Alan said. He looked at the woman and the dog, which was a sort of Jack Russell with a patch over one eye – it looked like the same breed he had seen with the mysterious figure in the field.

"The old cricket ball would be okay for Spey, but let's hang on to the photo," Alan said, popping it into a drawer.

That summer was devoted to improving the house. Alan's job as a photographer on the local newspaper, with the addition of the odd freelance wedding, left him little time for anything else but he felt fortunate to be doing something he really enjoyed and being paid for the privilege. Photography had always been his love.

A quarter of a mile from the back of the house, down in a dip, there were twin pools. Alan had fished there once as a lad. On a whim, in late September he decided he would take a gander to see if they were as he remembered them, as fantastic and as magical as his childhood memories. The last time he had been there, towards the end of the war, he was around twelve or thirteen, and he hadn't ventured back since.

He took Spey's lead from behind the kitchen door, walked out of the back gate of their house and into the first field, climbing a slight incline as he followed his memory's directions, Spey racing ahead. When he got to the second gate he could see there were bullocks in the field and decided it was wise to put Spey on his lead. The entrance to the field was a messy dried morass, covered in hoof prints, most of which were filled with water. However, the edges had dried out and were firm enough to take his weight. Alan used them as stepping stones into the field, shut the gate, replacing the blue baler twine that had secured it. *Don't want to upset the local farmers,* he thought.

The next field was empty, so Alan let Spey off the lead and the dog ran at speed, as if he could smell the water. The first pool was open, naked of trees about two acres, he guessed, the second slightly smaller, surrounded by trees, marsh marigolds and yellow irises. The last time he had been there was at least 25 years ago. Apart from the trees being much taller, the place had hardly changed in all that time and looked exactly as it had when he and his childhood mate Stevo had fished there. There was a stile into the wooded pool. Spey raced up and down the fence, looking for a way through.

Alan climbed over the stile, then let Spey through the trap at its foot. Alan thought there must be a shooting syndicate operating in the area, the trapdoor for the benefit of gun dogs.

Spey charged off around the edge of the pool, setting off a flurry of widgeon and mallard. Alan, trying to keep up, almost trod on a cock pheasant, sending the bird into a panic of flight and feathers and startling Alan's pulse rate into overdrive. He whistled and Spey came charging through the marshy ground at the pool's edge, flattening the vegetation and sinking up to his chest in thick black mud which oozed from the sodden moss.

Alan carried on squelching through the marshy ground, sometimes sinking halfway up his wellies, which prompted a graphic memory of the last time he was there with Stevo all those years ago and how on that occasion he had very nearly lost a boot.

Chapter 3

Alan's mind went back to a time after the war. Stevo had been told by a mate of his about this pool which was full of big perch, so the two boys had planned the expedition. They biked from the town up a lane to a large house called The Stables. Funny to think that years later it was destined to become Alan's home.

The two lads hid their bikes by pushing them into a huge laurel bush, untied their rods from their crossbars, and with bags slung across their shoulders they crossed the two fields towards the far pool. Under their arms they also carried two short planks, which Stevo had fashioned into crude paddles in the hope that the punt his mate had told him about did actually exist.

"That's the one," he said triumphantly, "the one with all the trees, my mate reckons there's a punt at the far end and we can use that to fish from."

As the pool was fringed with water lilies, a boat was essential. They quickened their pace, slithering and skating, sweating with excitement through the muddy surrounds of the pool. At the far end, up a narrow, overgrown channel, they found the punt, just as Stevo's mate had told him he would.

Great, this is where the adventure begins, Alan had thought then his heart sank, "But Stevo, it's locked."

"Bugger."

Sure enough, it was well and truly locked; there was a substantial padlock and chain securing the punt to a sturdy oak post.

Standing forlornly, gazing at the punt, Stevo leaned against the post. It moved a little in the soft, marshy ground. At this, the two of them pushed one way and then the other, and from side to side until, between the two of them, they were able to lift the post up. They pulled the looped chain with padlock down and slipped it under the post, placing it, with the padlock, on the end of the punt. They quickly threw their bags, maggot tins and rods onboard and Alan got in. Stevo gave the punt a big shove and jumped in at the other end. The pool was mirror-like and as flat as a pancake, making the paddling reasonable and progress easy.

Well out from the lilies, they settled down to their fishing, watching their porcupine quill floats sit up straight, clearly visible against the dark green, still water. After a short while, Alan's float lifted and lay flat on the water before returning to the vertical. With a long, steady pull, it slowly slid away into the dark depths. He lifted the rod, which bent towards a good-sized fish.

"Get the net, Stevo," Alan shouted.

He brought the fish to the net and Stevo lifted it into the punt, exclaiming, "What a beaut, got to be two pounds!"

They returned the fish and paddled to another spot where they both took and returned several lovely striped perch.

"Great, innit?" Stevo enthused.

Then, from the far side of the lake, they heard someone crashing through the undergrowth with breaking twigs and red-faced utterings.

Stevo said, "Pull your rod in mon, that could be Mad Hooky Mathews the keeper. Get paddling, we've got to get to the channel before he does."

With that they both paddled furiously in a splashing race to the bank, watching the undergrowth and the man spluttering through the soft surrounds of the pool.

Ashen-faced, Alan spluttered, "Who is he?"

"Tell you on dry land, just keep bloody paddling," Stevo replied.

They reached the bank and leapt out, running in the opposite direction of the man, who was like a demented hippo in hot pursuit. There were two loud bangs as he let go both barrels of a twelve-bore. The reports panicked the boys even further, injecting extra acceleration into their escape.

They ran through the marshy ground and Alan's right leg sank down almost to the top of his welly. He tried to heave it out and his foot came, minus its sock and the welly which was firmly in the grip of the bog and left in the stinking black mud. They squeezed through the fencing and hotfooted it until they had cleared the wood and made it up a gorse bank to a rise in the ground.

From their vantage point, lying on their stomachs, they could watch and see if the man was still following.

"I hope he dunner find our bikes," exclaimed Alan breathlessly, "and you said you'd tell me about the man."

"Well he's called Hooky, he's a sort of keeper," Stevo whispered, "and he's got a hook for a hand, bit like him in Peter Pan. My mate said he's mad and a right evil bugger."

"Wish you'd told me that before," complained Alan. "Why do they say he's mad?"

"Because he's a bloody nutter."

"I've got to get me my welly back or Mum'll kill me, she's only just bought them, she'll go bloody ballistic."

Stevo reassured him, "Dunner worry mon, we'll get 'em on the way back."

They waited until the watery sun started dipping towards the tree line before leaving their cover. Alan's foot was by now white and freezing cold. They walked tentatively back towards the pool, staying alert for a Hooky ambush, but there was no sign of him.

Only an inch of Alan's welly was showing above the mud. However, with some persuasion, it oozed out of the black, stinking goo. They found their bikes intact and Alan vowed he would never go there again, even though the fishing was ace.

Chapter 4

Many years on, at the very same pool, Alan wondered if Hooky was still about. *Probably dead,* he thought.

The sun was dropping, casting shadows across the water. As Alan rounded a thick coppice, he became aware of a presence. There was an older man standing still, silent and unshaven. He had a long dirty gabardine mac with a thick leather belt holding him together and baler twine around his trousers. He held a machete-type brushing hook in one hand and, as Alan's eyes strayed down his other arm they took in the fact that there was not a hand there but a hook.

After a sharp intake of breath Alan blurted out, "You gave me quite a turn." Then, in an effort to converse further or promote some sort of reaction from the silent figure, he continued, "It's really muddy down here."

In return, the man stared straight ahead, a glazed look on his hollow grey, unshaven face.

In a deep, guttural and somewhat frightening tone, he responded with just two words, "Thick mud."

Alan made a swift departure, muttering, "See you."

He called Spey and carried on round the pool. *Creepy,* he thought. It could only have been Hooky. Even as an adult, Alan was fearful. There was something decidedly weird about the old man and Alan felt like running as he had done in the distant past. As he reached the other side of the pool, he looked directly into the sun, which was blasting sharp light through the trees and dappling all in its path. Alan thought he saw the silhouette of another man, and a dog, on the other side of the lake. He turned away to call Spey and when he saw his dog running eagerly towards him he once again turned his attention to the vision across the water. Putting his hand to his forehead and shading his eyes against the dazzling light, he could now see there was nothing there. Had he imagined them? He didn't think so, and the figures did bear a resemblance to the man and dog he had seen in the field. He knew it wasn't Hooky; he could never have covered the distance around the lake and besides, he didn't have a dog.

Alan walked round to where he had, or thought he had, seen the man and as he got near, he noticed Spey down on his belly, as if someone or something was there. But the place was deserted and as the sun melted into the lonely landscape an unfriendly chill filled the air. Alan felt unease invading his body, making him keen to head home. He crossed the first field and called Spey, putting him back on his lead to go through the bullocks' field. The animals were on the far side and only raised their heads in a cursory glance before returning to their grazing. Alan tiptoed over the edge of the hoof prints in the gateway and looked up at the house, which had been enveloped by the descending blue-black darkness. The lights from the windows pierced the blackening sky, offering pinpoints of comfort.

After his meeting with Hooky and the vision at the pool, Alan was happy as he opened the door to the back porch and let Spey in. The porch had not been touched for years; perished plaster, peeling wallpaper and flaky ceiling making it ideal for housing a mud-caked dog.

"Stay there boy," he ordered.

Spey emptied his water bowl and flopped down with a thud into his basket.

Alan kicked off his wellies and walked through to

the lounge in stockinged-feet.

Donna was reading the evening paper. The children were watching a TV programme and without averting their gaze they muttered, "Hi Dad!"

Chapter 5

When Alan put the children to bed later that evening he said to them in a warning voice, "I don't want you two going down to the pools behind the house, not unless I am with you."

"Why's that, Dad?" Molly said excitedly.

He answered her query seriously, "There are some marshy parts there that you could sink into and the water is dangerously deep, so promise me you won't go down there."

Billy chipped in, "Yes, like quicksand, it will gobble you up and you'll never be seen again."

Alan admonished, "Okay Billy, we don't need your input, thank you very much."

The next morning, Alan kissed Donna on the cheek. "I'll take Spey for a walk and get a paper, do you want anything, darling?"

"Take Billy with you, Molly and I are making scones." Molly loved being in the kitchen alone with her mum.

On the doorstep there were two massive onions, the sort that win prizes at village shows. Alan went back into the kitchen. "He's been at it again, look at these two beauties."

There was a smell of autumn in the air as father and son walked down the lane. Leaves were blown from east to west and a cold wind rippled and rattled the tracery of branches. Spey raced ahead down the lane towards the allotments, where he went down on his stomach to the ground. As they turned the corner there stood a tall, erect man. He had kind, piercing blue eyes and was smoking an old cherry wood pipe.

"This err your dog, mate?" he asked.

"Yes," replied Alan emphatically.

"Well he's a real beaut."

Spey had wriggled across the tarmac into the shadow of the man so he could be stroked. The man bent over to fuss him and the dog's tail wagged furiously.

"He can take that all day," said Alan.

"Is this your garden?" asked Billy.

"Nope, I live down near the village, you can't miss it, it's the first in a row of cottages with a great big monkey puzzle tree outside."

Alan introduced himself with a handshake. "My name's Alan Tait and this is my son Billy."

"You're the new people up at The Stables. My name's Maurice Martin, although everyone calls me Mosser, so feel free."

Spey sat, taking it all in with his head cocked to one side. Alan looked down at the dog proudly. Spey's black and white coat shone and his eyes were the colour of clear best bitter. The dog looked up at Mosser, clearly trying to curry more favours.

Alan said, "Since we've moved in we keep finding vegetables left on our doorstep, don't suppose you can throw any light on it? It's a complete mystery to us."

"That'll be Digger, that's his allotment with the green shed. He started 'Digging for Victory' during the war and he's been digging ever since. Like me, he was excused enlistment in the war because we were both involved in essential agricultural work."

"What does he look like?" Alan asked.

"Well he's about five foot seven, got wispy, pale ginger hair, combed sideways to hide his baldness, a touch of the Bobby Charltons. Oh yes! And he doesn't smile a lot. He usually wears a sort of ginger herringbone jacket and dirty black wellies. You'll find him in the Cross Guns most nights, he sits in the window by the darts board, throws a mean arrow as well, so don't you get playing him for a pint."

Determined to know more about the village, Alan enquired about Hooky. "Do you know him?"

Mosser's whole demeanour changed. The smile disappeared and he said seriously, "Keep away from that one, he's bad news."

"What about the hook? Did he lose his hand in the war?"

"No, oh no, it was him having an argument with a threshing machine and the machine won hands-down. But seriously, keep the dog and the kids away from him, he's bitter and twisted, and he hasn't improved with age."

"Did you know the previous owners?" Alan changed the subject, aware of Billy listening intently.

"No not really, they kept themselves to themselves, although I did chat to the husband on occasions. Strange type though, bit of a townie, couldna make head nor tail on him. And she, well she was a brick short of a pallet! Reckoned she saw a man and a dog always staring at the house, looked like a soldier, she said. Reckoned it was the ghost of a man who had lived there in the past. Then she heard a man's voice on the baby minder, intercom thing. I said it must have been one of the taxi or the cop radios. He said his missus was getting upset, thought they were ghosts. I ask you - a dog ghost - the mind boggles."

"Yeah," Alan agreed, but underneath he knew it matched his own experience. He wouldn't own up to that though; he didn't want Mosser to think he was off his trolley too.

"Got to crack on," Alan said apologetically, "see you anon."

"Take care mate," Mosser shouted after Alan and Billy as they walked off down the last stretch of lane and on to the road to the village.

They came to the first row of cottages and there was no mistaking Mosser's house. As he had said, it had a massive monkey-puzzle tree in the front garden, dwarfing everything else. From the washing line down the side of the house, Alan guessed Mosser was a bachelor; the clothes were all male and they were thrown on the line in a way a woman would never do.

On the way back Alan, with newspaper clamped under his arm, looked over the fence at Digger's allotment. The seedbed was well raked, not a weed in sight, and the rows of plants were regimentally straight. The shed was painted forest-green and there was a water butt on the back corner. Spey lay in the long grass against the fence, his steaming tongue lolled out like a slice of pink Spam.

Billy said, "Look at those leeks, Dad, they're massive. How do they grow them like that?"

"Dunno," Alan replied, "Beats me, but I think that big heap of manure might have something to do with it."

When they arrived back at the house, Donna was still in the kitchen with her helper Molly, who was covered in flour. There was a lovely smell emanating from the Aga.

"What's cooking?" Alan asked.

Billy joined in, "Can we have some now? I'm starving."

"No, they're apple pies and they are heading for the freezer," replied Donna firmly. "Molly's made one herself, haven't you darling?"

"I inner going to eat that un," Billy blurted out.

Donna corrected him, "You're not going to eat that one."

"No," he replied, "I inner."

At this point Donna gave up her impromptu English lesson and went back to the cooker.

The next day, Alan had gone to work and the children were in school. Donna had the house to herself and was keen to get on with some improvement work. As soon as they had gone, she had begun getting the entrance hall ready for redecorating. With the aid of a wallpaper steam-stripper, she made short shrift of removing the layers of wallpaper that had built up over the years. The layers of different papers revealed how taste had changed; some of them didn't need much persuading and peeled off in huge dry stiff strips, some brought plaster with them. Under the third layer - a faded, rose pattern - she found the name *'Sam Leftwich'* scribbled with *'1937'* directly beneath it.

Sam Leftwich - same name as on the trunk, she remembered, *I wonder what happened to him? He could still be alive.*

On Alan's return from work, Donna proudly showed him her handiwork.

"Tidy," he said, "we'll have to do some replastering where it's perished, but all in all you've done a bloody good job."

"Look at this," she said, showing him the paper with Sam Leftwich's name on it, "Same name as on the trunk."

Alan looked at it with interest then apologetically he asked, "Mind if I pop down to the village for a pint?"

"Not at all, the kids have had their dinner so we can eat when you get back, it's only a cottage pie, didn't have time for much else."

"Sounds good. I won't be long – it's just I think I

know who's leaving our doorstep veg, he's called Digger. I thought I'd get him a pint; apparently he's in the Cross Guns most nights."

The sun was dropping, casting long shadows, as Alan set off down the lane. The smell of autumn filled the air as he stepped out purposefully at the thought of a pint

At the end of the lane there was a huge horse chestnut tree and all around, nestling in the grass and fallen leaves, were big, shiny conkers. It brought on immediate recall of his childhood.

I wonder if kids still play conkers, he thought and he stooped to select a few, admiring their shiny polished skins and pocketing them.

Chapter 6

Bert Grimshaw poked his head over his hairy grey ex-army blankets and peeped through his cobweb of threadbare curtains to see what the weather had in store for him. Something moved at the bottom of the bed and a little mottled and sleepy-eyed Jack Russell terrier emerged.

"What you doing down there, Dinks?" asked Bert.

Dinky responded to this by slithering, without standing, over to Bert. The dog lay on the man's chest and licked his stubbly chin. If there was ever true canine love it was Dinky's for Bert. But at that time of the morning, Bert was unresponsive to Dinky's advances. Instead he pushed the dog down the bed and, rubbing his eyes, sat up to look through the window.

Most villages have a Bert; someone who can brush hedges, cut grass, build walls, fix leaks, catch rabbits, repair farm machinery and, most importantly, make people laugh. Most of the time Bert rarely got out of his bib-and-brace overalls and he was always available for just about any job, big or small. Strictly for cash only. He was a great practical joker, pulling tricks like going into Digger's garden and moving all the plant markers in his beautifully prepared seed beds.

This morning, Bert was soon up. His trousers were hung up by the braces so that they looked like a paratrooper had dropped in during the night. He unhooked them from the door and stepped straight into them, pulling them up in one go. Sometimes even his socks were also included in this movement.

He went through to the bathroom with Dinky pitter-pattering across the patterned lino after him, eagerly waiting for Bert to take the lead from behind the kitchen door. Bert washed his top half with a flannel and, after a quick shave and brush-up, he slipped on his jacket and his army beret with its shiny North Staffs regimental cap badge, put the lead around his neck, locked the door, pocketed the keys, and set off with his partner in crime for the village shop.

The spring bell announced Bert's arrival. He greeted Madge Simpkins with, "What's the latest then, Maggie, got any gossip?"

"Well," she said.

"Well?" enquired Bert.

"Well," she agreed, "Charlie Wilkins was in half an hour ago, said he's got some work for you up at the farm."

Bert snapped back, "Why didn't the old bugger come to the cottage?"

"I dunno, anyhow he says he'll buy you a pint in the Cross Guns tonight some time between six and seven."

"Ah, well that's a different matter," he joked.

As Bert was in the pub every night, the arrangement suited him down to the ground. He left smiling with a copy of the *Daily Mirror* under his arm and a packet of crumpets in his pocket.

Bert didn't have much schooling but if they awarded common sense degrees at university, he would have passed with first class honours. There wasn't much he didn't know about country matters and he was a great historian to boot.

He remembered the old canal that ran through the village and the handsome strapping barge girls with long hair and healthy, brown complexions. They would give you a slap if you tried anything on and on many occasions Bert did come away with a stinging cheek and nothing else. All that remained of the neglected

31

canal now were waterless channels full of yellow irises, willow stumps along each side. Little hump-backed bridges, which once spanned the canal, now looked very strange, marooned in the middle of ploughed fields, landlocked and isolated.

In those days, between the wars, the village had its own railway station and youngsters would come on the train from the nearby town to fish for pike and perch in the canal. And the fishing was good. Bert remembered those days before the war fondly and often mourned them. The war had made a huge impact on him, but he didn't like to show it and, like so many of his generation, he didn't talk about it either. Sometimes he dreamed of his good friend Jabez cradling their dying friend Sam and would wake in a cold sweat. On occasions Bert wished he'd married, mainly for the company, but it was too late for him now and at least he was his own boss.

Bert had a devil-may-care attitude to life and always had a mischievous glint in his eye. His laughter spread throughout the village, as did his popularity.

That night, as instructed, Bert was in the Cross Guns early evening. He ordered his pint and sat in the window seats opposite Digger Owen.

"How's it going, owd lad?" he asked.

Digger, hardly cracking his face, said, "Canner complain mon, back's giving me some jip, other than that, not three bad."

At this moment Alan Tait pushed open the pub door and entered, walking across the stone flags to the bar.

The landlady, a small energetic woman with thick black hair, greeted him with a friendly smile.

"What can I get for you, my lovely?"

Alan hesitated as he scanned the beers on offer.

Bert interrupted, advising, "Try the Shires bitter, mate, it's the dog's bollocks."

Alan, carrying the recommended pint, walked over to Bert and Digger. "Okay if I sit here?"

"Pull up a pew, mon," said Bert hospitably.

There was no mistaking which one was Digger. The herringbone ginger jacket and the wispy hair combed sideways Bobby Charlton-style were a dead giveaway. Mosser's description was spot on.

"You must be Digger?" Alan enquired.

"How do you know that?"

"Mosser told me, said you always sit in the window," Alan thought it wise not to mention the lack of smiles, or the hairstyle.

The bar door opened and a draught was followed by a big man - almost as wide as he was tall, with a florid complexion and a veined nose that betrayed his liking for ale.

Bert called out, "'Owdo Charlie me old mucker, 'ow's it going?"

"Too much work and not enough hours in the day," Charlie said.

As soon as Bert had seen him he had downed the rest of his pint and plonked the glass down with an audible bump, where it was clearly visible.

"What's your poison, Bert?" Charlie said.

"Pint of the Shires, sir." He tended to call people Sir if they were buying him a pint.

"What about you, Digger? Charlie added.

Alan interrupted, "I'll get Digger's."

"Yo dunner 'ave to do that mon."

"Well I'm sure it's you who has been leaving fruit and veg on our doorstep."

"What of it?" Digger mumbled. "I just dunner like

waste and besides, you've got the wife and them young 'uns to feed."

"Well it's very kind and much appreciated," Alan said, "and you can't get veg as good as that at the supermarket."

All four sat around the table, with full pints.

Bert said "This 'ere's Charlie Wilkins, he farms up at Wheat Hill."

"Pleased to meet you, my name's Alan."

"Where do you hang out then mon?" Bert asked.

"We've just moved into The Stables, top of Long Lane."

Bert, with a surprised expression, said, "A good mate of mine, Sam Leftwich, used to live up there, got killed in the last war, not long after D-Day at the Battle of Caen. Bloody crying shame, he was a great bloke, our RSM he was, salt of the earth were Sam."

Alan said, "Well that's funny, we found an old travel trunk in the attic with his name on it, nothing much in it - just an old cricket ball, bails and a stump."

"Sam, well Sam he were a good cricketer, captain of the village team an' all and played for the county sometimes. I know he got a hat-trick against the league champions."

"I wouldn't mind betting them bails and ball were from that same match," interjected Charlie.

Digger nodded in approval, uttering, "Ah he were a good 'un."

The landlady joined in. "He were a right good looking bugger an' all."

"You had your eye on him then did you Doreen?" said Bert laughingly.

She responded loudly, "Cheeky bugger you are, Bert, I were only a nipper then wunner I, cheeky sod."

Charlie said, "I'll have to shoot, lot to do. Oh yes!

Bert, come up to the farm with them ferrets o' yorn, we're over-run with rabbits, there's loads down along the edge of the wood below the twelve-acre turnip field."

"Can't come tomorrow but I'll be up day after, early."

"So long lads," came Charlie's parting shot, "Nice to have met you, Alan."

Alan suddenly felt at home in the Cross Guns, as though he'd been a regular for years, so he drank another pint then said, "Better show the wife a good husband."

Bert smirked, "Do you know one, mon?"

Alan went to the door, "Cheerio, see you anon, thanks again for the veg, Digger."

"Now dunner you go buying any sprouts, I've got some beauties coming on, just like the Cartwright twins at number 12, tight little buggers."

Bert looked astounded; Digger was not given to displaying much humour.

Alan strode up the road and into Long Lane. He put his hand in his coat pocket to check that his Olympus Trip was safe; he usually carried this smaller camera with him in case the unexpected happened.

He was looking towards his house, silhouetted against a dramatic sky; a huge Prussian-blue cloud stretched from north to south with a slash of pastel blue highlighting the skeletons of the naked trees as they lost their leaves. He took his camera out of its case, steadying himself by leaning on a fence post, and took several shots as the sun dipped dramatically into night. He shuddered with the cold, put his camera into his pocket, and blew warmth into his cupped hands.

When he walked in through the front door, Molly was waiting excitedly. "Dad, Dad, we're doing the story of Bethlehem at school and guess who's playing Mary? You know, she's Jesus's mummy."

"Now let me see, could it be someone called…" he paused, "could it be Molly?"

She jumped up and put her arms around his neck, screaming, "Yes! It's me Dad, me! And guess what, Billy didn't even get a part in the older kids' play."

Donna said, "I heard that Molly, don't be unkind to your brother."

"Alright," Molly conceded, adding, "but he is a big head."

"What did I just say?" Donna exclaimed.

"Alright," Molly whispered to Billy, "But you are, you are, big head, big head!"

He responded by saying, "At least I'm not a daft girl and I dunner wanner be in a stupid play anyhow," at the same time pinching the back of Molly's arm.

She cried out, "Mum!"

The next day, Alan left for work early as he had a heavy workload. He arrived at the office and went straight to the darkroom to develop his SLR film. Having done that he decided to develop the film from his Olympus Trip.

Some stunning shots came to light; the sun had dropped just behind the trees and the last drop of light warmed the front wall of his house. But he noticed something very odd. In the field he could make out a blurred image of what looked to be a man and a small dog. He was sure there had been no one there when he took the shots but, although quite indistinct, those two figures were definitely visible in the picture. He looked at it closely, then he put it under a grant projector and enlarged that section of the photograph. He could see the pair were very similar to the figures he had seen before and, even more oddly, none of the other pictures had the man and the dog on them.

He was fascinated and wanted to know more. The Stables was a very old house and he started thinking of ghosts. Maybe a footman had been murdered there. All sorts of ideas entered his head.

In the evening, Alan showed Donna the photographs. On seeing them she enthused, "They are beautiful, that one would make a super Christmas card."

"But just look at this one," it was the one with the blurred image of the man and dog.

Molly, looking over their shoulders, said, "That's him, Dad, the man with the dog, the one I saw in the field, that's him."

Billy mocked, "She's off again."

"Well you can see them, can't you?" Molly said angrily.

"Stop arguing, you two," said Donna, "Yes, you can see them, although not that well. He does look like a soldier."

"But," Alan said, "you're missing the point. When I took those shots there was no one in the field."

"You must have missed him," said Donna.

"No, there was no one around, the place was as deserted as Aberdeen on flag day."

"Don't forget, you'd only just left the Cross Guns," Donna joked.

Autumn gradually fell into winter. The house was taking shape and Christmas approached. The days shortened and grew ever colder. Alan didn't mind the cold, but he deplored damp foggy mornings and rain. However, whatever the weather, Spey had to have his morning walk and he let them know by standing next to the door where his lead hung. When Alan took it down the dog jumped and spun around excitedly.

"See you in a bit, darling," Alan called as he left the house and walked down the lane. He edged through a gap in the hedge and jumped the ditch on the other side. Spey raced off, sniffing along the hedgerow. A little way off, a small terrier appeared. Spey was jumping from side to side in an effort to induce the small dog to play. They were a distance away but he saw the smaller dog disappear as quickly as it had appeared, through the hedge, and it was gone.

I can't be sure, Alan thought, *but that looked just like the dog on the photo. Very interesting.* However, logic convinced him otherwise; it had after all been only a fleeting glance and no doubt just a coincidence.

Back at the house, after a cup of tea and a slice of toast, Alan was ready for work.

Donna asked, "Can you drop the kids off at school today?"

"Of course," he replied.

"Oh yes, and see if you can get some logs, it gets cold later on."

"Bags I'm in the front," Molly chirped when they got to the car.

"No! Me!" argued Billy.

"Stop fighting, you two. Molly, you're in the front."

"That's not fair," Billy groaned. "Why her?"

Not being able to come up with an adult answer, Alan simply said, "Because she bagged it first."

After dropping the children off, Alan drove into town, arriving at the office, which was already buzzing with activity, phones ringing, and the tapping of typewriters.

Later that day, when he had a spare minute, Alan went back into the darkroom to look at the negatives he had developed. When he found the one with the man and dog on it he held it up to the light but there was no man or dog on the negative. He printed it again and there once more was the faint image of the two figures. He showed the negative and the print to Arthur, one of the compositors.

"Must be another neg," Arthur observed.

"No, here's the neg and there's the print."

"Crazy," said Arthur.

"I know, it's got me baffled," Alan said. "It doesn't make any sense at all."

He clipped the negative and the print together and put them in his wallet.

On the way home, sleet blew horizontally and the wind lifted the few remaining leaves into the chill of the night. Alan fancied a swift pint at the Cross Guns and thought he could use the seeking of logs as an excuse when he got home.

Not that I need an excuse, he told himself.

He pulled up on the car park and could see Digger in his window seat as usual.

Chapter 7

Once in the pub, Alan saw Bert was also present. He and Digger were laughing, coughing and spluttering.

Alan went to the bar. "Evening Doreen, it's horrible out there. Pint of the usual, please."

He watched the beer rising up the glass, forming a nice head. Picking it up, he took a long slurp and went to join Bert and Digger. "What's the big joke, lads?"

"Well it's like this. Next village up, the Church Warden, Chubby Challinor, did a big clean-up in the churchyard - yer know, pruning and all that," Bert's story was interrupted as Charlie Wilkins entered the bar. Bert waited till Charlie had joined them before continuing his story, "Chubby then piled all his brashings on the waste land outside the church and set fire to it. Had a right good bonfire, he did. Well, when it were reduced to a patch of ashes, Rupert Wilkinson – the vicar - turns up and parks his car where the bonfire had been. Then…"

"You'll like this bit," chipped in Digger.

Bert continued, "The vicar comes out of the church and sees his tyre is on fire. So he thinks by driving it off he could put out the fire. In fact, it had the reverse effect; all it did was create a draught, which really got the fire going. Poor old Rupert jumped out of the car and watched it burn till there were nowt left but the shell."

Charlie by now was crying, leaking laughter tears which ran down his florid face. He took a large paisley-patterned handkerchief from his top pocket, mopping up the tears and blowing his nose. His face reddened further as he spluttered, "Bet he thought it was Ash Wednesday."

Bert said he took a lot of ribbing, "Yer know, 'ashes to ashes' and the like and 'Vicar, I think you should fire Chubby'."

Talk of fires reminded Alan of his quest. "Anyone know where I can get some logs?"

Bert without hesitation said, "Jabez! Gittins, he's a good mate of mine, we went through the war together, he'll sort you out. He's a great bloke, tell him I sent you."

"Where does he live?"

"Well when you're going into town, there are several white smallholdings. Jabez has the second one along, on the right."

"Thanks for that, I know where you mean. Right, better get cracking. Cheerio, see you soon."

The kids were in the lounge, arguing as ever, and Donna was in the kitchen. "I've done a beef cobbler."

A bit of comfort food, can't wack it, thought Alan. "Lovely," he enthused.

Over dinner he told Donna about the burning car and the vicar. "Bert's told me where to get logs so I'll call in tomorrow on the way to work and order some. Lovely dinner by the way. Where's Spey?"

"I took him for a walk and he's flat out in front of the fire. Fancy a glass of wine?"

"Love one."

"Get me one while you're at it, there's one opened in the fridge." Donna grinned. "Molly is really excited about being Mary in the school play. Oh yes, I keep forgetting to ask, are your mum and dad coming up for Christmas?"

"Dunno," Alan replied.

"Well give them a ring."

"I'll do it tomorrow."

"Why not now?" she asked.

"It's cheaper from work, I don't pay."

"You're a tight bugger, Al."

The next morning, Alan was up early, promising Donna he would sort the logs out as he kissed her on the cheek.

He came off the bypass, turning left and following the road into town. He came to the second house in the row of smallholdings. Turning off the road and up to the white five-bar gate, he left his car and went through the smaller gate to the right, walking down the gravel drive. The white painted house and garden were neat and tidy.

To his right was a well-manicured lawn. He followed the small path alongside it up to the house. The front door was a deep burgundy colour with brass door furniture which had been polished so that it shone in the early morning light. Lifting the heavy knocker, which was in the shape of a leaping trout, Alan let it fall with a resounding bang and then felt embarrassed at the volume of it.

He could see some movement through the dimpled glass and the door was opened by a handsome woman, her dark hair held back by a floral scarf and her hands covered in flour, further smudges adorning her cheek. Smells of baking and autumn fruits came from the kitchen and the interior of the house looked as pristine as the outside.

"Morning," the lady greeted him with a warm smile.

"I'm looking for Jabez Gittins, have I got the right place?"

"Yes you have, I'm his wife Laura, you're not selling anything are you?"

At this point she offered a floured hand and shook

Alan's. "No, I'm after some logs and Bert Grimshaw thought Mr Gittins could get me some, is he in?"

"Yes, he's right down the bottom with the pigs, you'll recognise Jabez, he's the one with the hat on. And call him Jabez, not Mr Gittins," she advised, "he prefers that."

Alan walked down the side of the house. Everything was in order; an orchard stocked with apple, pear and plum trees, a long covered storage area with logs stacked up neatly. After going through the gate he could see a man leaning over a big sty, emptying food into the troughs. There was a distinct smell of cooking swill and pigs. A sheepdog started barking and a Jack Russell terrier ran up to greet Alan, sniffing at his trouser leg, no doubt scenting Spey.

"Mr Gittins," Alan said.

"Aye," he looked up and replied, "but call me Jabez."

The collie eyed Alan and decided he liked him. The dog was predominantly black, but had one side that displayed the blue merle in him, having one bright blue eye and one brown. This gave him a slightly mad look, and with a white streak that went from between his eyes and over his left ear, it reminded Alan of Melville's Captain Ahab from *Moby Dick*.

"Bert Grimshaw sent me," Alan said, "thought you'd be able to get me some logs, said to mention his name."

"How is the little bugger? Haven't seen him lately, yes I can get you logs."

"Bert seems fine, how do the logs work out?"

"Well see that pick-up yonder? I'll fill the back of that for five quid, how's that?"

"Great," enthused Alan.

"I'll pop them up Saturday morning around ten," Jabez said, "where do you live?"

When Alan gave him directions and told him the

house was called The Stables, a faint look of surprise crossed the man's face.

"My best mate lived there, we went through the war together but Sam didn't make it, got killed at the Battle of Caen after D-Day. Bert was with us as well, all in the same regiment. Sam who lived at your house was made up to RSM of the regiment. He had a natural leadership quality, you know. I rose up to the dizzy heights of corporal. Bert was with me when Sam bought it. Tough little bugger, Bert, went all through the lot without getting a scratch."

As Alan drove on into work, he tried to imagine Jabez and Bert as young men during the war and what they had been through - the trauma of losing a close friend. In some ways he sort of envied them the adventure of it all. But then he suspected that in reality it would have been pretty horrific and not how it was in the films.

On the Saturday morning it was a crisp day, a gentle northerly breeze making it cold. Donna was upstairs and saw Jabez's pick-up coming up the drive.

She shouted downstairs, "Al, the logs are here."

Alan went out to greet Jabez, Spey and the children inquisitively joining him.

"Bit of a sharp 'un this morning, where do you want the logs, mate?" Jabez enquired.

"Just dump them right there, I'll sort them out later," Alan replied.

"Some good oak and there's some cherry as well, smells great when it burns, well seasoned an' all," Jabez informed.

Billy, keen to please, said, "Can I help, Dad?"

"Yes, go and get the wheelbarrow, it's down behind

the greenhouse, and bring it here and start filling it."

"Okay," Billy said and disappeared down the garden. He returned with the barrow and a beaming, triumphant grin.

Whilst they were still unloading, Billy was filling the wheelbarrow with logs and quickly complained of cold hands. He left the barrow where it was and went indoors, rubbing his hands.

The two men finished unloading just as Donna came out with two mugs of coffee. "Do you take sugar, Mr Gittins?" she asked.

"No thanks," he replied, "and please call me Jabez."

Spey did his best to get Jabez's attention. He brushed up against his trousers, wagging his tail. Jabez bent over and stroked the dog. "He's a beaut, I've got a soft spot for collies, too intelligent for their own good though, if you ask me. Well I'd better push off now, still got a bit to do."

Alan handed him a five pound note saying, "Are you sure that's enough? There seems to be an awful lot of logs there for the money."

"Get away with it, I'm more than happy with that."

"Well thanks very much," Alan replied. "Why don't you pop up to the Cross Guns sometime and I'll buy you a pint? Bert would like to see you, I'm sure."

Under the end bedroom and the bathroom there was a large covered area, no doubt where they used to keep the carriages in the old days. Alan called it the harness room. He swept along one wall and then stacked the logs against it, finally standing back to admire the neatness of his efforts. There was a side door into the kitchen so that if the weather was bad there would be no need to go outside for wood.

Ideal, he thought.

Chapter 8

On a cold morning in the second week of December, the sky looked heavy enough to fall and the clouds had a dirty yellow tinge to them which in Alan's mind signified snow. He kissed Donna on the cheek. "It looks like snow, I'll see you tonight."

"Drive carefully, oh and see if you can find somewhere we can buy a Christmas tree."

As he drove off to work the odd snowflake landed on his windscreen and a childlike excitement crept in; he secretly hoped it would develop into a full-blown snowfall. All through the day it continued. Tiny snowflakes, which hardly qualified as snow, were accompanied by a very low temperature.

Junior reporter Emily Longhurst came into Reception as Alan was leaving. She wore a long navy coat with a fur-trimmed hood and the cold had blushed her cheeks, which Alan found very attractive. He banished such thoughts as he reminded himself that he was very happily married, but as he drove home he carried a vision of the attractive Emily.

When he got to the village his car automatically veered to the right, onto the car park of the Cross Guns. Inside, Bert and Digger were in their usual place, along with a round, hirsute, jolly-looking man. He wore a black waistcoat which only covered the top half of his belly, so that his braces were visible. His face was reddish-brown and his nose edging towards a dark shade of purple.

"Evening Doreen, pint of Shires please," Alan ordered. He then joined the three older men in the window seats.

Bert said, "It's a bit Pearl Harbour out there inner it?" Seeing Alan's puzzled expression he explained, "A bit Pearl Harbour, you know a nip in the air."

Then he introduced the third member of the party, saying, "This un's Nicker Stevens who lives in one of the estate cottages and this here is Alan who lives up at The Stables. If yer missus and kids want a Christmas tree at the right price, Nicker's your man."

Alan smiled, it was good to be in the right place at the right time.

"You after a tree then are you, mate?" Nicker enquired, "What sort of size?"

"Well around seven foot would do the job."

"And do you want it sawn or with roots?"

"What's the difference, price-wise?"

Nicker said, "With roots there's a small surcharge for three cartridges."

Seeing the puzzled look on Alan's face, Bert explained, "Nicker goes round in the daylight and fires three shots into the ground at the base of the tree, then after dark he just goes back and lifts it, pops out like a carrot, dunner it mon?"

Alan said, "Can we have one on the Saturday morning, Christmas week?"

Nicker quickly replied, "Oh you canner have it in daylight."

"Is this legal?" Alan asked.

"Well to the letter of the law, strictly speaking it inner, anyhow I'll drop her off soon as it's dark," he replied.

"OK," said Alan, "see you then."

Alan left for home. The sky was leaden, heavily pregnant with snow. When he got home he went straight to the harness room and under a couple of empty tea chests, one containing Trotsky - who didn't appreciate being woken from his slumbers - he found his old toboggan, covered in dust and cobwebs.

Alan had made it when he was but twelve years old but it was still serviceable and its name was still visible in crude lettering along each side. *Speedwell.*

Great, he thought and went out and back in through the front door.

Donna said, "There's been some funny sounds coming from the harness room, go and have a look."

"No need," said Alan, "it was me looking for my toboggan."

"You bloody idiot, why didn't you tell me you were home? It scared me half to death." He simply said, "It looks like snow tonight."

"Did you ring your parents to see if they are coming for Christmas?"

"Yes! Day before Christmas Eve, all things being equal."

The next morning, a Saturday, quietness descended over the house and garden, which were muffled in a thick blanket of snow. Alan drew the curtains. It was a white-over; a deep crisp four inches had covered everything, even sticking to the washing lines and piling up deep on the top of fence posts. Trotsky was treading tentatively towards a blackbird that was sending showers of powdery snow off the pyracantha to get at the profusion of berries which lay beneath.

As the children awoke they piled into their parents' bedroom in a mayhem of excitement.

"Dad, look outside!"

"I know, I've already had a look," he said.

"Can we go tobogganing?" Billy shouted. "Can we, can we?"

"Hang on kids, let's gets dressed first," said Alan, "it's not going anywhere, it's still snowing."

He went to the bathroom, followed by his pleading children.

"We'll get some breakfast then we'll see, go and get washed and put warm clothes on."

In the kitchen, Donna had a big pot of porridge simmering on the Aga.

"Thought this would give you inner warmth," she said, "at least that's what it says on the adverts."

Billy and Molly were straight down to breakfast, washed and kitted up for the cold. Donna instructed them to take off their balaclavas while they ate.

"Honey or golden syrup?" she enquired. In unison they agreed, "Syrup please, Mum."

They liked the syrup because they could pour it from a height, making a window so they could see the design in the bowl through the syrup. Quickly polishing off their porridge, they were soon outside, Billy shouting "Come on Dad!" as he pulled the toboggan down the drive and into the lane. Theirs were the first footprints in the deep virgin snow. Spey ran amok, jumping the fence and running in circles with his nose to the ground, sniffing everything.

Down the lane, Alan lifted the toboggan and dropped it over the fence into drifted snow in the field. The children got through as Alan held the wires apart with foot and hand. As they crossed the field, Alan could see footprints coming from the opposite direction. On closer inspection he could see there was one adult's and a small dog's prints in the deep snow. There was something very strange about these tracks; they stopped suddenly in the middle of the field opposite Alan's house and there were no signs of them leaving that spot.

Mad, he thought. He could come up with no logical answer, unless the person had walked backwards using the same tracks, carrying the dog. *Crackers.*

"Come *on*, Dad!" the kids called, "What are you looking at?"

"Oh nothing," he said though Spey too took a keen interest in the spot where the mysterious tracks ended.

Alan put Spey on the lead as they went through the gate into the next field. There were sheep, looking almost grey against the blinding whiteness of the snow, feeding on turnip tops that were peeping out. Screams of children enjoying themselves broke the silence and on the skyline they could see the silhouettes of a crowd.

The children ran ahead, leaving Alan to drag the toboggan up to the edge of the hill. There, the snow was well compacted, making it ideal. Down the centre of the hill it was like a sheet of solid glass. Alan suggested Billy go down first, but only on the side where it was somewhat slower. All the while, Alan's mind kept drifting back to the footprints in the snow. He was totally baffled. *It's got me beat,* he thought, *bloody odd.*

The children were tiring and he suggested one last run with all of them on the same toboggan. He trusted old Speedwell would take the strain as he lay down headfirst and the children lay on his back.

"Now hold on," he said and he asked a muscular youth standing by to push them over the edge on the fast centre run. It had been years since Alan had done this and his excitement and enthusiasm bubbled over as the three of them thundered down the icy centre at speed. Alan and his Speedwell stood up to the test. The kids screamed all the way down, Spey giving chase, barking excitedly until Speedwell came to a grinding halt.

The children whooped, "That was ace, Dad, shall we do it again?"

"No, we'd better get home. But don't worry, the snow's going to be here for some time."

On the return journey home, Alan pulled the toboggan by its now frozen rope and the two children trudged behind, complaining that they were cold. It started to snow heavily, big flurrying flakes, tickling their eyelashes and sticking to their clothes and noses. When they got back to the first field the two sets of footprints had all but disappeared and Alan put them to the back of his mind.

In the house Donna said, "Get those wet things off and put your gloves on the Aga."

"My nails are hurting, Mum," complained Molly.

"It's only your circulation returning," Billy said, turning to Donna, "Dad's old toboggan went like a bat out of hell, and he took us all down on his back."

"Yes, it was fandabidosy," added Molly.

"You kids go into the lounge. There's a nice fire, but don't get too close or you'll be getting chilblains."

"What's them, Mum?" Molly asked.

"They're not very nice, that's what they are. This snow's set in, good job you got those logs sorted," Donna said to Alan. "Did you see that man and his dog on the field earlier? He was stood looking towards the house just after you left, I thought you were bound to bump into him."

Alan didn't bother to tell her about the trail of prints as it seemed unbelievable, even to him, and he had seen it with his own eyes.

Chapter 9

At the beginning of Christmas week, Alan went into town on the bus for a reunion with some of his childhood mates. This was a yearly ritual which he always enjoyed.

When he entered the bar at the King's Arms there were just two members of his childhood gang already there. Clive, a privately educated man, now working in sales, and Grinner, a gas board stoker.

"Get yoursen a pint Al, and give us a tenner for the kitty."

As Alan waited to be served the rest of the boys, amid much laughter, turned up. Wacker, the tallest of the group - a thin wiry electrician, and Terry who was always ready with a joke or a story and had a permanent grin etched on his face. Two more tenners went into the kitty and two more pints were pulled by Jackie, the well-endowed barmaid.

The same old stories dominated the conversation; the good times, their transgressions and adventures were all recalled during their second round. Old dog-eared photos of their childhood were taken from wallets as Jackie came to clear the empties from their table.

"Excuse lads," she said as she leaned over to pick up the empties.

Terry quipped, "See you've got your bingo top on then, Jackie."

"What do you mean - bingo top?"

"Eyes down, look in," he said mischievously.

"Cheeky bugger you are, Terry Griffiths," she said as a rosy flush covered her face. "If I didn't have my hands full I'd give you a smack."

"I'd love that," Terry's grin widened.

They settled down to some serious drinking and the stories and reminiscing got into full swing.

"Remember Clive's dinghy?" chipped in Grinner.

They were transported back to childhood, after the war. Clive had unearthed a big rubber dinghy from his dad's garden shed. He reckoned it had come off a Lancaster bomber and by the number of patches it had, it must have been machine-gunned a few times. How to inflate it would prove difficult but some bright spark suggested taking it to the County Tyre Company.

The boys had set off on a bright spring morning, carrying their great tangled lump of patched rubber. It was a unanimous decision that Clive with his private school accent should approach the manager, Mr Fulton.

They dragged the dinghy up to the double doors. Mr Fulton came out from his cubbyhole, puffing on a pipe.

Clive, using his posh voice, asked, "Mr Fulton, can you blow this up for us, please?"

The man sent smoke signals from his pipe, "No problems, how's your dad?"

The lads stood in an expectant semi-circle as the valve was connected to the airline. As the rubber wrinkles smoothed out and it began to take shape, Grinner exclaimed, "Cor, it's big inner it?"

The excitement spread throughout the tiny band when inflation was successfully completed. As one, they thanked Mr Fulton.

"You're very welcome lads, anytime as long as we're not busy," he replied smilingly.

They had carried their new launch down the side of the building, past the old mill and towards the brook, which meandered through lush meadows at the bottom. They soon discovered the best way to carry the dinghy was for them all to be underneath, with Clive at

53

the front, his head outside, directing operations. They looked like a giant beetle as they crossed the field toward the launch site.

The beetle trampled through the watercress beds and up to the edge of the brook. On arrival the water was bank-high, in spate, and going at a great rate of knots.

Terry, for once without a smile on his face, said, "Do you think it's safe?"

Wacker said, "Course it is, piece of cake, who's going in it first?" There was a deafening silence. Employing Wacker logic he said, "Well, it's Clive's boat so he should have the honour of going first."

They all agreed, nodding their heads.

"Yes Clive," said Grinner.

Clive, with a look of pride etched on his face, sat in the dinghy as they held it in to the bank with a short rope. They passed him the crude paddles then let go of the rope and launched, the boat spinning out into the fierce current. Clive, flailing at the water with his paddles, went into a flat spin, out of control and in the grip of the fast current.

The launch hissed and lost air and the sides of the dinghy gradually came in while the bottom began to collapse and, like the *Titanic*, it began to sink. Heroic Clive, like all good captains, stayed and went down with his ship. He then rose up like a phoenix, making a desperate dive towards the bank, rope in hand and grabbing at the bankside vegetation. Wacker grabbed the rope and pulled the crumpled launch onto the grass while Clive dragged himself up the bank, wet and mud-splattered.

Following his launch up the bank to safety he said, "That was bloody ace, lost the oars though."

"They were crap anyway," Grinner chipped in.

The boys took the dinghy and themselves to their homes after what had been an adventure they wouldn't forget. Clive took a real dressing-down from his mother, but he thought to himself that it was all worth it.

The next time the dinghy surfaced was in the summer, on the river in town. This time more patches had been applied and the main river was in a kinder mood. Lime trees lined the bank and damsel flies danced; iridescent blue, bars of colour in the sun. The lads lay on the mown grass with their dinghy all set for its second launching.

This time confidence was high and the water low as they plopped the dinghy into the river. They all followed it in with a variety of jumps and dives and pushed it out in front of them to mid-stream. They pulled themselves into the dinghy, slithering in like young white seals then standing, diving, swearing, and causing waves of bubbly hilarity.

The bridge upstream was festooned with multi-coloured bunting and numerous flags fluttered in the light breeze. Further up they could see lots of well-dressed people on the balcony of the boathouse. The sounds of laughter and the clinking of glasses flowed downstream.

Clive, with his private school knowledge, said, "Of course it's Regatta Day, we'd better clear orf."

Wacker responded with, "Bollocks to that, we're having a good time, they don't own the river."

A loudspeaker request ordered, "Will you please clear the water, we're about to start the first race."

The lads ignored this and instead all tried standing, hands linked, around the edge of the dinghy, before falling, splashing and gurgling bubbles of laughter into the water.

The speaker boomed out again, "Will you clear the water, you're the scourge of the river."

The consensus of opinion was 'not a cat in hell's chance' and the boys continued their joyous splashing.

The regatta folks then sent a single sculler downstream, requesting they 'Get orf the river and go to the bank'.

The reply was an emphatic, unanimous, harmonious, "Piss off!"

The sculler retreated back upstream towards the boathouse like a pond skater, the lads triumphantly cheering his retreat. Terry, in his home-made swimming costume converted from an old pullover, stood up, his white body quivering, exclaiming triumphantly, "That showed the posh bastards!" while giving them the V sign.

More loudspeaker orders followed and were duly ignored. Wacker said, "Look here, look what's coming now."

Creating a big bow wave, what looked like a whaler boat was being powered by what appeared to be half the bloody first fifteen rugby team. They surged menacingly towards the boys and their dinghy, scattering swans and ducks in their wake.

The boys all agreed that discretion was the better part of valour and kicked out toward the bank, nosing the dinghy in front of them. Once safely up on the bank they all flicked Vs at the whaler's crew who responded by shouting, "Get orf, you're a damned nuisance!" as they turned back upstream.

Now adults but with childhood memories that united them, other stories were told and often altered and embroidered to the point of legend.

When Terry went on to order yet another round,

however, Alan half objected, "I'd better think about going."

"Jackie will ring you a taxi, won't you darling?" Terry suggested

"I'll ring you a taxi Alan, but for your information I'm not your darling, Terry Griffiths."

"Okay! But you know you've got a soft spot for me," he replied.

Wacker chipped in, "Yes, quicksand."

Jackie rolled her eyes and left them to it.

"Your taxi is here, Alan!" Jackie yelled from behind the bar.

He shook hands all round and wished everyone a happy Christmas. In the taxi he looked across at the driver. He was a stiff, erect, well-built man; Alan guessed he must be near retirement age, and he had some sort of foreign accent.

Alan asked him, "What part of the world did you come from originally?"

"Germany," was the sharp response. "I was a prisoner of war and when it all ended I decided to stay here, haven't been back to Dusseldorf since."

That was that. The man didn't seem to want to pursue the subject and fell into a sullen silence, concentrating on his driving as sleet splattered the windscreen, his wipers going at full tilt though fighting a losing battle. When the taxi turned off the main road into the lane leading home and leaving the street lights behind, darkness fell, highlighting the sleet.

Alan was looking forward to supper as the taxi slithered up Long Lane.

"What the bloody hell was that?" the driver said in a shocked, chilling voice.

Alan said, "I wasn't looking, what was it?"

The driver seemed genuinely concerned, "There was a man and a dog right in front of us, I saw them in the headlights for a split second and then nothing, and I didn't hit anything."

"Was the dog small?" Alan encouraged.

"Yes, yes, a little small dog, do you know them?"

"Well sort of, in a way, but not very well really."

Back home, Alan wished the driver a happy Christmas and a safe return journey, watching as the car's lights disappeared into the dark night.

His sleep that night was somewhat disturbed as the man and the dog invaded his dreams and he wondered exactly what the driver had seen.

On the Saturday evening, about an hour after dark, there was a knock on the door and there stood Nicker, wrapped up against the weather with a khaki scarf wrapped high around his neck and across his mouth and nose. On his head, a ratting hat perched at a rakish angle.

"Come in," Alan suggested.

"No, I canner stop, got more trees on board, pay us in the pub later," Nicker said as he scurried up the frozen drive where he had left his vehicle.

Alan gave the tree a good shaking before dragging it into the hallway.

Donna, seeing the tree, exclaimed, "What a beauty, lovely shape!"

Spey sniffed all around the tree and the children, full of excitement, said, "Can we put it up now, Mum?"

"No you'll be off to bed soon."

"Oh Mum, can't we?" they groaned.

"No, we'll do it tomorrow when we've got all day and it's something for you to look forward to."

After the children had gone to bed, Alan and Donna put the tree up, ready for decorating the next day. They stood it in an oak barrel planter and steadied it with several carrier bags of sand. It was sited in the dining room, against the tall window so that it would be seen inside and out.

The following morning, the children excitedly decorated it, all the decorations ending up on the front of the tree and low down, where they could reach.

Donna leaned back, hands on hips. "Looks good," was her satisfied closing observation, "it's a lovely tree."

Mid-afternoon on the day before Christmas Eve, Alan's parents arrived, their old faded yellow Volvo Estate drawing up at the front door. Alan went straight out to greet them. It was cold with a north-easterly wind whipping up the top surface of the powdery snow, making mini blizzards.

"Come on in, I'll get your cases, didn't think you'd make it."

Frank, Alan's father, said, "The main roads are fine, it's just the side roads that are a bit dodgy."

Donna came into the hallway, greeting them with big hugs. "I expect you'd like a cup of tea?"

Her mother-in-law, Maud, replied, "Lovely, I'm parched and we didn't want to stop en route in case we couldn't get started again. Where are the kids?"

"They are watching *Mary Poppins* in the lounge, go through."

The fire was blazing, sparks flying up the chimney, and the whole room shimmered with pleasing patterns from the open fire. Spey was fast asleep on the fireside rug, Trotsky curled up next to him, enjoying the direct heat. Neither of them moved to greet the visitors.

On seeing their grandparents, both children leapt to their feet and greeted them momentarily before Billy said, "Do you mind if we finish watching this?"

The grandparents in turn said that was fine as they plonked themselves down on the huge settee with sighs of tired satisfaction.

Donna brought in tea and a plate of home-made mince pies. "Turn that down Billy, don't you know it's rude to watch telly when you have visitors?"

"They're all right," Frank said, "They did ask us if it was okay."

"Alright, but sit a bit closer and turn it down."

Donna treated Alan's parents as if they were her own. Her father - a fleet air arm pilot - was shot down off the coast of Malta, machine-gunned in a dinghy after ditching his aircraft in the sea. The German pilot had flown back over her father and machine-gunned him while he had floated defenceless; his co-pilot had survived to tell the story. Donna still held a deep-rooted dislike of all things German and never forgave them for depriving her of a much-loved father. A few years on, her mother had re-married and she and Donna's stepfather had moved to County Mayo on the West Coast of Ireland, so contact was minimal.

Maud exclaimed, "Yummy! Lovely mince pies, Donna, you really have a light touch when it comes to pastry."

Frank added his praise to his wife's. The long drive and the direct heat from the fire soon made his eyelids heavy and they started to flicker like the fire, before eventually they closed. Soon he was fast asleep, his head thrown back, snoring contentedly like a great bear who had feasted on honey. Maud and Donna tiptoed out to the kitchen and Alan, like his father, drifted into a comfortable half-sleep.

A while later, Maud woke the men with a cup of tea. "Donna wondered if you two would like to go for a pint before dinner?"

Alan responded, "Wonder no more, right Dad?"

Maud ran them into the Cross Guns in the Volvo, saying as she dropped them off, "You'll have to walk back or get a taxi, Donna and I are going to crack a bottle of wine."

Frank took his golf umbrella from the boot and they walked into the bar purposefully. There was quite a crowd there in the dim light; Digger was as usual in his window seat with Bert, Nicker and Jabez.

Alan greeted Doreen, "Evening Doreen, six pints of Shires please."

"Do you want a tray, love?"

"I'd better, thank you."

Frank carried his own pint and Alan placed the tray in front of Digger.

"What's this all about then, mon?"

"Well one's for you for the veg, one's for Jabez for the logs, one's for Nicker for the tree and one's for Bert for, well for being Bert. Cheers and happy Christmas." Alan added, "This is my dad, Frank. Dad, this here's Jabez, Digger, Nicker and Bert and that's Bert's dog, Dinky."

The men all shook hands and Frank toasted, "Happy Christmas, lads!"

There was much clinking of glasses, "And many of 'em."

Frank said to Bert, "I see from your cap badge you were in the North Staffs."

"Ah, for my sins I was, bloody good regiment though."

Jabez jumped in at this point, "Yes, us two were in it together."

"Yes, if it wunner for me and Jabez the bloody war'ud still be going on," chirped Bert.

Nicker joined in as he brushed froth off the tip of his nose, "Dunner listen to Bert, he's a right bullshitter."

"Ah and Digger dug for victory and he's still doing it, dunner know the war's over, see."

"No seriously, we lost some good mates, one of them was Sam Leftwich our RSM, he were in your son's house and you'd go a long way to find a better bloke, solid as a rock he were," Bert told Frank.

Doreen collected glasses from their table and Jabez said, "Same again Doreen, one for the ditch, boys!"

"I was in the Durhams," said Frank as he tackled another pint, "saw a bit of action but was invalided out with suspected TB in 1942, could have been a blessing in disguise. Bloody good pint this Shires, could become a habit, but we're going back home day after Boxing Day."

Alan enquired, "Did your mate Sam have a dog?"

"Yes he did, why do you ask?" Jabez said.

"No reason really, was it a Jack Russell though?"

"Yes, Patch was a Jack Russell, in fact Patch is an ancestor of my terrier, and of Dinky."

Alan pondered this for a while as they slurped the last of their beers and headed for the door. "See you anon, if not sooner."

As Alan and Frank left the pub, very fine soap powder-like snow was blowing in all directions. They walked close together under the gaudy protection of Frank's massive golf umbrella and frozen puddles cracked under their tread.

At The Stables, the girls were sitting looking into the fire, nursing glasses of red wine and in deep conversation, which was interspersed with the odd giggle.

Donna said, "Can you get your own tea? The casserole's in the slow oven and there's some mash on the top, just heat it through and help yourselves."

Alan and Frank ate at the kitchen table on the end nearest to the Aga. Alan poured them a bottle of beer each and they ate enthusiastically. After their late dinner they joined the ladies in the lounge, keeping the fire well banked up and talking long into the night.

Outside, the snow fell lightly onto the silent landscape and so Christmas looked all set to be a white one as the temperature plummeted to crystallise all it touched with a shivering sparkle.

Chapter 10

The morning of Christmas Eve, a low sun crept across the crystallised snow, up the side of the old house and in through a gap in the curtains.

Alan drew them wide, "Gorgeous morning, I'll take Mum and Dad a cuppa."

The children were down in the kitchen when Alan put the kettle on the Aga.

"Shall we go tobogganing?" they both pestered.

"No, we've got loads to do to get ready for tomorrow."

"Oh rats!" said Billy.

Alan knocked on his parents' bedroom door. Maud was sitting up, but his dad, head covered, was snoring under the duvet. Maud shoved him.

"Tea's up!"

"What, who, when, where?" Frank hauled himself up into the upright position "Tea, oh yes, great."

"I've left your teabag in the mug, Dad, I know you like it like bull's blood. I'm off to work shortly, but finish at lunchtime so we can pop down for a quick pint later."

Maud said, "That's all you two buggers think about."

Alan planted a peck on her cheek, "See you later, Mum."

As Alan was about to leave, Donna said, "Your mate has been round."

She held up a complete plant smothered in tight green sprouts.

"Lovely," said Alan, "We've got chestnuts. See you this afternoon, tara a bit, see you later."

It was a quiet morning in the office. Someone had brought in a ruck of mince pies and these, with a few drinks intermingled, resulted in not much work being done.

Emily Longhurst sat on a high swivel chair, sipping red wine, her long legs tapering down to high-heeled ankle boots.

Alan couldn't help thinking, *Now that's the perfect way to fill stockings* - as, most likely, did most of the men in the office. It crossed Alan's mind that he shouldn't be harbouring such interest, but he justified it to himself that as a photographer his interest was purely artistic.

Most of the younger lads in the office were besotted with Emily and they kept her glass full. They surrounded her like the proverbial bees round a honey pot. She was dressed primarily in red and with tinsel in her hair she looked the epitome of Christmas and happiness.

"Want a glass of wine, Alan?" she offered.

"No thanks, I've got the car. Anyway, I'm off now, have a good one."

On his drive home, Alan's thoughts kept drifting back to Emily's long legs. *I suppose if you stop looking you're dead,* he thought, but at the same time he tried to erase the image. He counted himself lucky to have Donna as his wife, but Emily's legs were something special, aesthetically pleasing and a joy to the eye, something to be admired. It was impossible to ignore them.

When he got home his dad was eagerly waiting, asking, "When are we going to the pub? I'm dehydrating, Mother's volunteered to take us down but we'll have to walk back."

"Sounds good to me," Alan enthused.

When they entered the Cross Guns, the usual gang were in the window seats, plus Jabez Gittins who was bellowing a great belly laugh at one of Bert's stories.

Alan ordered the pints, saying to Doreen, "Love the tree, it's a beauty."

"Yes, we like it," she replied, "Nicker Stevens got it for us for a few free pints."

Even the pub's tree was, true to the supplier's name, nicked.

Watching Jabez and Bert, Alan imagined them as young soldiers during the war and wondered what horrors they had gone through together. There was a natural bond between them, one born out of experience and mutual admiration for each other's qualities, although if you had described it in such a way, the response would be, "Bullshit, we're just good mates."

They reminisced about the war, but it was always the funny stuff and Frank joined in, revealing a side of his father that Alan was unaware of. Like the night they were billeted in a French brothel where the sleeping arrangements were interesting to say the least, and tins of bully beef bought a few extra privileges.

Back at The Stables, Donna was bedding down the children, hanging their stockings and instructing them on how to behave prior to Santa's visit. "Now if he comes, keep your eyes tight shut or he might not leave anything."

Billy had long since stopped believing in Father Christmas but he had been warned by his parents not to spoil Molly's belief in, as he put it, 'that load of old codswallop'.

"I've left Santa a mince pie and a glass of whisky outside the door," said Donna.

Downstairs, Maud was enjoying a glass of Amontillado by the fire when a dog barking broke the silence. This was followed by a whistle and some scuffling footsteps, muffled slightly by an easterly wind which was growing in strength. Maud looked at Spey who was growling softly with ears pricked and head cocked to one side.

"I've got the kids settled," Donna said as she came in the room.

"Are the boys back?" asked Maud.

"No, I don't think so."

"Funny, I heard footsteps and someone whistling outside."

Ten minutes later they heard the front door bang, followed by laughter. Frank and Alan pushed open the lounge door and came in giggling like schoolboys.

"Sounds like you two have had a good time," Donna observed.

"Yeah," said Alan, "that Bert is a witty little bugger and he's got some great stories. Whether they are true or not is another matter."

"Did you come up earlier?" Maud enquired, "I heard footsteps and a dog outside, thought it was you two."

"No, not guilty. Didn't see anything out there, how many of those have you had?" Alan quipped, pointing at the sherry glass in his mother's hand.

They all sat down by the fire, the wind buffeting the house and rattling the windows. Occasionally the fire smoked from a downdraught caused by the wind cutting horizontally across the chimney pot.

Chapter 11

The night of Christmas Eve, Alan lay in bed, unable to sleep. The wind howled but beyond it he heard the village clock striking three am and he slipped out of bed and padded to the bathroom. He thought he heard a whistle, but put this down to the wind as it surrounded the house, making bizarre banshee sounds. As he passed the children's room, he spotted the mince pie and whisky Santa should have had. He drank the whisky and put the mince pie in his bedside cabinet then he slipped back into bed and snuggled up to Donna, his thoughts again turning to Jabez and Bert together in battle. He eventually went to sleep dreaming about the war.

Christmas morning was bright. There was a thin smattering of overnight snow and a heavy frost which crystallised the air and painted crazy intricate patterns on the windows.

Molly burst into the bedroom shouting, "He's been, he's been, and he's had the mince pie and whisky!"

"Yeah," Billy said. "I went to the bathroom in the night and my stocking was full and so was the whisky glass. Strange that, he must have gone and come back to finish off his drink."

"It's only 6am," Alan complained, looking warningly at Billy, "don't wake Granny and Grandad, will you? They need the rest."

Spey came into the bedroom and, as was his habit, leapt onto the bed and stretched out so that his front paws were just under Alan's chin. He put his cold nose against Alan's cheek, making him recoil.

At 7am the eighteen-pound turkey was put into the Aga and Donna had a huge gammon joint on the table.

She had criss-crossed the fat to make a diamond pattern and was pushing a clove into each cross. She then spread a mixture of marmalade, honey and Dijon all over the outside.

"That looks gorgeous," Alan commented, "good enough to eat."

As Donna went to the fridge, Alan pinched a loose piece of ham from under the joint and hurried into the hallway to devour it.

Gradually the house came to life. The children came into the kitchen, asking when they could open the presents under the tree.

Alan said, "Patience, not yet. Creep upstairs and see if Gran and Grandad are awake."

"They are awake, I could hear them talking," said Billy.

Molly complained, "Spey has been eating the chocolates off the tree."

Alan made mugs of tea for his parents and took them up into the bedroom, asking if they'd like him to draw the curtains.

After they had enjoyed a full English breakfast they went into the lounge and Alan rattled the poker in the fire. It had been banked up with wet slack the night before and it soon burst into life. They sat down, the two men nursing a cup of coffee and a glass of Glenmorangie, and the ladies with small sherries - as had always been their family tradition on Christmas morning. All the presents were brought into the lounge and opened enthusiastically, wrapping paper going in all directions with lots of *oooh*s and *aaah*s.

Spey foraged through the papers in case something edible had been overlooked. As Molly had warned, he had managed to eat most of the chocolates from the lower branches by sucking out the contents, leaving the foil wrappers hanging limp and empty.

Billy went upstairs and came back down in his brand new Liverpool FC kit with his new football, saying, "Dad let's have a kick around outside."

Molly stopped dressing her new doll momentarily, enthusing, "I'll come and play, Billy."

He emphasised his disdain, "You canner play footy with a girl."

Donna ordered, "It has been snowing, so you can both stay in, it's far too cold to play out."

Christmas evening was devoted to watching the usual Christmas offerings on telly: *The Benny Hill Show* and *Zulu*. Full up with Christmas dinner, chocolates and nuts, all of them drifted in and out of red-cheeked slumbers in front of the fire. They all finished off with a port and some cheese and crackers, Alan commenting, "I'm not really hungry, but that ripe gorgonzola needs eating."

In bed, Frank and Maud agreed it had been a lovely Christmas Day, while outside the very fine snow was swirling around the old house, sticking to the windows.

Maud whispered, "It's a nice house, but do you think they have taken on too much? There's a lot of work to do."

Frank murmured, "You're forgetting they are young."

He turned over, taking half the covers with him, and was soon snoring, mouth open and gone to the world.

On Boxing Day morning a watery, insipid sun tried its best to thaw the frozen landscape. Alan was the first to rise; he looked through the window and could see wood pigeons standing awkwardly, flapping on his purple sprouting, nibbling the heads and stripping the leaves before either had a chance to develop.

Once downstairs, he filled the big flat-bottomed kettle and put it on the Aga. Billy came into the kitchen, tousle-haired, proudly wearing his Liverpool shirt.

Alan said, "It looks like you've slept in that shirt, son."

Billy smiled, saying in a matter-of-fact way, "That's 'cause I have."

Gradually, voices and footsteps could be heard murmuring through the house, until the whole family descended into the warmth of the kitchen.

Donna was putting all the leftovers into one bowl; potatoes, stuffing, sprouts, parsnips, carrots and chestnuts.

"That's going to make a great bubble and squeak, I can hardly wait," said Alan.

"Yes, I almost prefer Boxing Day food to Christmas lunch," said Frank, "Are we going to the pub at lunchtime?"

"I think there's a good chance, Dad."

After a long, slow breakfast and several cups of coffee, they put on warm clothes and it was decided that the whole family, including the dog, would walk down to the Cross Guns. Billy carried a football and Spey ran ahead as if he was pleased to have such a large audience to his athletic prowess. He jumped in and out of the wood, scampering through the undergrowth and sending the powdery snow flying in all directions then running back up the lane, as if to say 'What did you think of that then?' and also to ensure they were following him.

"What a gorgeous day," Donna remarked.

There was a pale blue sky, although the wind from the east was stiffening. On the grass patch opposite the pub there were lots of children of all ages playing with brand-new footballs, while others sat astride shiny new bikes, watching.

The pub was packed with all types of people; youngsters home from university, visitors like Frank and Maud, and, of course, the regulars. Bert Grimshaw, complete with mistletoe optimistically tucked behind his regimental cap badge, greeted Alan, "Happy Christmas mon, I take it this is your missus… or perchance someone else's?" he grinned.

"You've met my dad and this is my mum Maud, and my wife Donna."

"Pleased to meet you all. Jabez is in the window seat with his wife and Digger, come over and join us."

Donna sat down opposite Digger and complimented him on his vegetables and generosity.

A smile lit up his face. "No bother, Missus."

Alan thought Digger should smile more often; it totally transformed his lined face from his usual hound-dog look, so that the creases became laughter lines.

Alan hardly recognised Jabez's wife Laura as she looked very different dressed up. Although middle-aged, she was still very attractive. Alan thought she must have been an absolute stunner when she was young.

Laura whispered to Bert, "I invited Mary, but regretfully she said she didn't feel up to it and declined."

"That's a shame, she's a lovely woman," was Bert's sombre reply.

Laura explained, "Mary is the widow of Sam Leftwich. They lived in your house for a number of years - lovely people, devoted to each other. Such a shame she never got over it."

Donna said, "I'd love to meet her."

"I'll sort something out," said Laura, "when the weather's a bit better. Jabez will run her over, I'm sure she'd like to see the house again."

Charlie Wilkins, red-faced and buttoned up in a quilted jacket, jostled his way over to the group and there were more handshakes and season's greetings.

"Can I get anyone a drink?" he enquired.

There was only one empty glass and that was Bert's.

"I can drink a pint of Shires if you twist my arm."

"Never guess who I've just seen walking up the village," Digger said.

"Who was it then?"

"Owd Hooky, he dunner get any better looking, dirty owd bugger."

"He's a dodgy one, that un," Bert chipped in, "yo dunner want anything to do with him."

Alan responded, "Yes I know, Mosser was telling me all about him, said to keep dogs away from him."

"He's always skulking around those woods back o' yorn place, down by the twin pools," Charlie informed. "Dunner often see him in the village."

Alan told them the tale of him and Stevo, the welly and the shotgun blast when they were kids.

"Yeah, he's a right fruitcake, that one." Charlie added, "Some people reckon it was him who shot Sam and Mary's dog Patch during the war."

Digger chirped up, "Yeah, I remember that an' all, it was around the same time as Sam bought it in France."

"It were me who found the dog, poor little bugger," said Charlie.

Donna, Maud and Laura Gittins hit it off and were deep in conversation. Donna enquired again about Mary Leftwich, expressing a wish to meet her.

73

"I'll give you a ring and you can come down one afternoon," said Laura.

The pub was gradually emptying. Billy and Molly came into the bar.

"We're hungry, when are we going?" asked Billy.

"In a few minutes," said Donna.

"One for the ditch, Alan?" Bert suggested.

"No, we'd better get off to lunch."

"Under petticoat rule then are we?"

"No," said Alan, "just bloody hungry."

They said their goodbyes and walked up through the village and into the lane that led to The Stables. There was no traffic about and Spey ran ahead.

Frank shouted after him but Alan said, "He's alright Dad, he knows the way home."

Although it was very cold, most of the snow had gone, replaced by a heavy hoar frost which kept the landscape in suspended animation and highlighted delicate spiders' webs spun into the naked hedges.

As they came up alongside the wood, Spey jumped the fence, sniffing around the base of an old gnarled oak tree. There were several dead branches covered in green lichen.

Alan said, "I'll have some of that wood for the fire." Having straddled the fence, he picked up a branch and threw it out onto the drive.

"Can we come over?" Billy asked.

"Yes, but mind the barbed wire." Grandad Frank lifted him over and he started helping his dad to get the branches onto the drive.

Donna said, "It's too cold to hang about, we'll go and start the lunch."

She and Maud walked one each side of Molly as the sun began to cast long low shadows down the frozen drive to the house.

Frank offered to get the wheelbarrow so they could cart the wood back to the house. Spey was scratching at a log, trying to get under it.

Billy helped, lifting the branch and revealing a flat piece of stone underneath. "Dad, look at this, there's summat here."

Alan brushed the earth and leaves away. It was a grave; a carved flat stone about one foot square which read 'Patch R.I.P. cruelly killed 1944'.

Just then, Frank plus barrow trundled back up the lane, but as it was getting progressively colder, they called it a day. He lifted Billy back over the fence and followed him. On the lane, Alan and his dad smacked the branches on the tarmac where they broke easily so that they would fit into the fireplace. The occasional one when smashed to the ground failed to break, sending shockwaves up their arms, like when a cricket ball misses the meaty part of the bat.

Having filled the barrow, the three of them pushed it up the darkening lane, the wheels cracking the frozen puddles in the potholes. They could hear a dog barking in the wood but saw nothing. The barking soon diminished and faded into the distance.

They left the logs by the front door and stamped their feet. Frank rubbed his hands and snorted like a water buffalo, exclaiming, "It's really putting it together out there."

Billy asked, "What do you mean, Grandad?"

"Well you know, getting frosty and colder," he explained.

"Lunch is ready," Donna shouted through.

"Good, I'm starving," came an unrehearsed chorus.

They all sat at the kitchen table and feasted on turkey, ham and a massive pan of bubble and squeak.

Billy was foraging in the pan with his fork.

"What are you doing?" asked Donna. "Do you want some more?"

"No, I'm looking for chestnuts."

A jar of home-made green tomato chutney was demolished, followed by a bottle of claret.

That night the whole family sat in front of a roaring fire, watching television whilst imbibing the spirits of Christmas in the warm, flickering room.

After a quick breakfast the next morning, Frank and Maud were ready for the journey back home. There were kisses and cuddles all round.

"We've had a super time, thanks for having us," Maud said.

"Drive carefully, Dad, the road's not all that bright," was Alan's parting shot.

Soon the faded old Volvo, packed to the gunwales, was out of sight.

After bacon butties all round, Alan said, "Now kids, put on some warm gear and we'll go and take a butcher's at the grave we found. Are you coming sweetheart?" he asked Donna.

She answered by getting her anorak out, saying, "I'll be with you in a jif."

She ran upstairs and came down in faded jeans and a massive sweater which reached halfway down her thighs, more like a dress. As a family, they walked together along the lane to the wood.

"That wind's bitter," observed Donna as she zipped up her anorak as high as it would go and brought her scarf up to cover her nose. "Are you kids okay?"

"Yes," said Billy, "but you said it isn't right to call children 'kids'."

"Well it isn't, unless you happen to be their mother and in a hurry."

When they arrived at the wood, Alan produced two plastic carrier bags.

"What are they for, Dad?" asked Billy.

Alan proceeded to wrap the bags around the top strand of barbed wire, which adequately demonstrated their protective purpose when getting over the fence. They all negotiated the barbed wire, but Alan lifted Molly over. Spey had already jumped across, with an easy vertical take-off, and was excited that the whole family was joining him.

Looking at the grave, Molly observed, "It must be a dog's grave."

Billy blurted out, "Course it's dog's grave, whoever heard of a bloke called Patch, dopey?"

"Well it could be a Mr Patch. One of our dinner ladies is Mrs Patch, it could be a relation."

Donna interrupted, "We know it's a dog's name, but there's no need to speak to your sister like that."

They pulled all the weeds and brambles away to uncover the tablet properly and read the inscription once more.

Billy asked, "Was he killed in the war?"

"I believe he was killed while the war was going on," said Alan, "but not in the actual war."

"I'm going to bring some spades up when it is a nice day and really tidy it up and put some flowers on it," said Molly.

"What for?" asked Billy.

Molly, with a serious look, said, "Well I just think it would be a nice thing to do, someone must have loved that dog to have made a gravestone for him."

"I agree," said Alan, "we'll do that one day soon."

The wind grew stronger and had a damp edge to it.

The family turned back towards home. Spey as usual led the way. Crows were blown like flapping black bin bags across the grey sky, with twigs and other debris airborne in the swirling gusts of wind.

A week of rain turned snow to slush and dispersed the last remnants of ice. In the hedgerows and the skeletal wood, snowdrops poked their optimistic heads towards the light, signalling the oncoming of spring. By mid-March, the season was well on the way, green shoots apparent all over the garden and the hawthorn blossom starting to burst into life.

Chapter 12

Alan loved this time of year as it bore optimism and the oncoming of the trout season.

Spring was in the air when Nicker turned up with a trailer and deposited a huge mound of horse manure on the side of the drive. On seeing Alan he said, "Get that dug in mon, it's some good tack, you could eat it. It's well rotted, but you need to get it in the ground."

"What do I owe you for that lot?"

"Gie us a quid mon and see us alright for a pint. It dinna cost be owt, just a bit of digging."

The following weekend a pick-up came up the drive while Donna was pegging out the washing with the help of Molly.

"Go and tell Dad, Jabez is here," Donna said then shouted, "Morning Mr Gittins!"

"I've told you it's Jabez," he replied then called out to Alan, "Morning! I've got a few leftover logs if you fancy 'em, but the real reason I'm here is I was wondering if you fancy a bit of fishing next Thursday, trout season opened Monday?"

"Great, I can manage that, Thursday's fine, I'll look forward to that," Alan enthused.

"I thought we'd try Corve Brook, it's a great little fishery," Jabez suggested, "one of my mate Sam's favourite haunts, some lovely wild browns."

In the evening, Alan tidied up his fly boxes, arranging all the flies in neat rows. He cleaned his floating line and stretched it, to avoid great loops of line flopping onto the water.

Thursday duly arrived and Alan was up, dressed and ready for the off. From the landing window he watched the drive in excited expectation. Smack on

7am, Jabez's pick-up swung in. Alan bounded downstairs and out through the front door.

"Morning Alan," Jabez greeted him, "stick your gear in the back."

Alan placed his tackle bag, waders, rod and landing net in the truck.

"Pull that canvas over your stuff in case it rains, although it doesn't look like it will."

Alan ran back into the kitchen and kissed Donna quickly on the cheek as the children were dawdling down the stairs.

"Have a nice day, darling," Donna shouted after him.

After the three-mile drive they could see the brook through the trees to their left. It looked at a perfect level, and at its champagne-bubbly best.

Crossing a small single track bridge, they parked on the grass verge opposite a small white-walled cottage. In the garden was a sign which read *'Private Fishing Corve Anglers'*.

They knocked on the studded oak door and it creaked open.

"After day tickets are you lads?" He was a friendly-looking, squat, solid man, bald-headed with a small neat beard. He wore moleskin trousers held up with braces, over a lumberjack-type shirt.

Jabez enquired, "How's it fishing then Andy?"

"Anner had many about yet but I think they've been getting a few."

They put on their waders and with rods, bags and nets they set off downstream. It was a beautiful day; a gentle westerly wind put a nice ripple across the water. They came to a white post and Jabez explained, "This is where the fishing starts, I'll kick off here and fish the top half. Downstream you'll come to an old wooden seat, you start there and fish the bottom half right down to the end of the beat, it ends at the big pool at the confluence with the little brook which comes in on the far bank."

Alan adjusted his bag on his shoulder, "What fly are you starting on?"

Jabez said, "I've always done well with a Wickhams Fancy. We'll meet up again at the bench, should be around 1pm."

"So long, see you later, tight lines," Alan set off.

The older man watched as Alan walked off purposefully and it reminded him of Sam before the war. A sadness descended over him. He missed his old mate, but he was pleased he had met Alan and had someone with whom to share his passion for fly fishing.

A moorhen busied itself in the rushes on the far bank as Alan tentatively entered the water, exploring the shingle bed of the river. It was ideal for wading. He worked line off his reel, watched it drift down with the current, then lifted his rod and made the first cast of the new season. He watched his line snake out straight and tidy but with some coils caused by the long winter on the reel. His fly landed lightly on the water under the far bank.

He fished and waded, covering all possible lies, but there were no takers. He changed flies from the Peter Ross he was fishing to the Wickhams Fancy Jabez favoured. It wasn't long before he felt that gentle tell-tale tug, like a muscle in the current. He lifted his rod and he was into a fish, the first of the season.

When it came to the net it was a full-finned brownie, a multi-spotted fish around about half a pound.

He said out loud, "You're too pretty to knock on the head," and carefully lowered it into the water where it shot off sulkily to the depths downstream.

Alan left the water and ate half of one of his corned beef sandwiches. Gradually he worked his way downstream. Covering every inch of the water, he took two more lovely brown trout which he also returned.

He came to the confluence and the large pool which signalled the end of the beat. The currents were hard to read and seemed to be going in all directions due to the incoming brook. He cast across and, although he was fishing with a floating line, the current pulled it back and it gradually sank.

Whilst deciding on what to do next, he was drawing line up into his hand when there was a solid tug and a fish exploded into the air. Alan hand-stripped the line and then let the fish run and take up the slack so that he was able to get the line back onto the reel and take control. When it came to the net, he was surprised to see that it was a rainbow - a good two pounder in lovely condition. This one he despatched and, wrapping it in a damp cloth, he put it in a plastic carrier and placed it in his fishing bag.

He looked at his watch. *Perfect,* he thought. It was ten to one and there was just time to walk back to the bench and meet Jabez. He trudged back upstream and, as he approached the bench, he could see Jabez sitting examining his fly box.

Alan made his presence known, "How did you get on?"

Jabez looked up. "Had some great sport on the stretch between the trees, difficult casting though. What about you?"

"Three brownies which I put back and, surprise, surprise, a rainbow, which I knocked on the head." Alan took the fish from his bag to show the older man.

"It's a fine fish," Jabez said, "lovely condition, full-finned, obviously an escapee from the hatchery up that side stream."

The two men sat eating their sandwiches and swapping fishing stories. The day was fine and the men totally at ease in spite of their age difference.

Jabez, scanning his fly box, picked out a small fly. "Try that one on your dropper, it's a fly tied by my old mucker Sam Leftwich. What he didn't know about fishing wunner worth knowing," he enthused.

"He was killed during the Battle of Caen wasn't he?"

A silent sadness spread visibly over the older man's face and Alan felt embarrassed that he had asked.

Jabez reached out with a tattooed forearm, his big cracked, shovel-like hand held the tiny fly with great delicacy. "It's a variant of a Greenwell spider," he said, "works a treat, give it a go." He poured coffee from his flask, took a sip and continued, "Sam was a great fisherman, in fact he was good at everything he turned his hand to. Cricket, football, fly-tying, fishing and good at being a friend. Solid character all round."

Alan wanted to know more about Sam but curbed his inquisitiveness as he felt it was neither the time nor the place. Instead he said, "I'll go up to the top of the beat and fish back to here and you do the bottom section."

The two men went in opposite directions. Jabez shouted over his shoulder, "See you back here about four, that is if you fancy a pint on the way home."

Alan shouted back, "Is the Pope Catholic?"

A couple of hours later they were back at the bench.

"That spider worked well on the dropper, got lots of pulls, great sport," Alan enthused.

Jabez had two nice rainbows from the bottom pool and they both agreed it had been a great day to start the season.

They walked back upstream to the pick-up, where they took off their waders and put them with their tackle in the back, covering them over once again with the canvas sheet. Jabez drove along the lanes, back towards the main road, but he turned down a lane that looked little more than a farm track. At the end they came to an open area with three houses and a pub which looked closed, although there was smoke curling up out of the main chimney.

"Is it open?" asked Alan.

"The Bricklayers Arms never closes."

Leaving the pick-up on the grass at the front of the pub they pushed the archaic front door open and smoke billowed out. Inside resembled someone's sitting room rather than a bar. The interior was dark and there were two men at the bar; one tall and gaunt with curly black hair, who banged the bell on the counter, took his pipe from his mouth and shouted, "Des, you got customers."

The landlord duly appeared, scratching at the space between the top of his trousers and the bottom of his grubby pullover. "What's your pleasure, gents?"

The other customer, a man as short as he was round, with a face covered in stubble - giving him the appearance of an over-ripe gooseberry - chipped in, "Try the Boningales, it's a cracking pint."

Dutifully, Alan and Jabez took his advice and stood at the bar. Jabez took about a quarter of his pint in one guzzle and said, "You're right mate, that's just the ticket."

They took their pints to a table nearer the open fire.

"It's funny," said Jabez, "fishing today I felt my old mate was with me."

"Is that Sam Leftwich you're talking about?"

"Yes," Jabez replied, "it's like you hear voices but

it's the water running across the shingle, daft innit?"

"No," said Alan, "I've experienced the same on the Spey in Scotland, it's weird."

"Sam taught me to cast a fly line," said Jabez.

"Well having seen you cast, I'd say he did a bloody good job."

"He'd bark out instructions, I always remember him shouting, 'It's a fishing rod not a bloody magic wand'. Even to this day, when I'm tired, if my casting gets a bit ragged I say to myself, 'Jabez, it's a fishing rod not a magic wand'!"

This was the first of many fishing trips for the two men, who became good friends, on equal terms, their age difference of little consequence. Alan gleaned bits of information about Sam and was keen to know more but never liked to push it, as a sadness swept across Jabez's face whenever his old friend was mentioned. It was as if Jabez blamed himself for being alive, as if somehow he had let his friend down.

Chapter 13

On the way back from a fruitless sea trout fishing trip to Wales, Alan and Jabez called in at a pub in a forgotten area of the borders. A buxom, chatty barmaid pulled their pints and they sat on an ancient settle in front of a scrubbed table which had been scoured to such an extent that the nails stood up like proud shiny silver nipples against the bleached wood.

"Nice drop of ale this is, lad," Jabez said smilingly as he wiped the froth from the end of his nose.

Alan said, "Did I tell you about the grave we found at Christmas? In the wood next to our house, it says 'Patch' on it."

"Ah yes, that'll be Sam and Mary's little Jack Russell. We all think that bastard Hooky shot him. We were in France at the time; coincidentally it was around the time Sam himself was killed. I'm glad you found it, I had a look a couple of years ago, but couldn't remember where it was."

"It was fairly well concealed under fallen wood and leaves. Spey, my dog, uncovered it and Billy helped me to clear it."

"Lovely dog was Patch," said Jabez, "It's a good job Sam wasn't around at the time or Hooky would have been in big trouble, Patch was Sam's soulmate."

"We found a photo too, in our loft - of Mary and Patch." Alan went on to tell Jabez about the photo he had taken of his house and of the strange image of a man and a dog. "Next time I'm in the pub I'll bring it to show you."

When Alan pulled up at Jabez's smallholding, he was unloading his gear when Laura came out. "Hang on Alan, I've got summat for you."

She went back into the house and when she

reappeared she was carrying a large pie. It was topped with deliciously brown pastry. Alan thanked her as he placed it carefully onto the passenger seat.

On a perfect late spring day, Jabez had been working, cutting grass and doing his edges. He was finishing off by feeding the pigs. The sweat was running off his forehead and into his eyes, making them sting so he wiped his face with his handkerchief and sat at the bottom of his garden in an ancient deckchair. The sheepdog lay in the grass and went to sleep, the brown eye firmly shut but the blue one occasionally flickering open, to keep half an eye on the world.

The terrier jumped up into Jabez's lap and tried to get comfortable between his legs.

"Settle down Churchill," Jabez muttered.

Soon all three were slumbering in the warm spring sunshine, floating somewhere between dreams and reality. Jabez dreamt he was on a riverbank in Wales, changing a fly on his cast. Looking downstream, he could see a fisherman casting across the current, dropping his fly gently into the gurgling water just short of the far bank. The man turned and looked back at Jabez. It was his mate, Sam Leftwich, with a smile on his handsome face, waving.

The terrier was dreaming too. His muffled bark and twitching legs woke Jabez, who was happy until reality struck home and he knew that Sam would never cast another fly. Jabez felt downcast as he rose and ponderously walked back towards the house, analysing his dream. He put it down to his fishing trips with Alan and his talking about Sam.

As he walked into the kitchen, Laura looked at him. "Are you okay dear, what's up?"

"Nothing," he replied, "it's just me being silly,

nothing to worry about."

Laura could read her husband like a book. She cheerily said, "Sit down, I'll make you a cuppa and there's some scones straight out of the oven, would you like one?"

Armed with a hot scone, spread with farm butter and his favourite home-made damson jam, Jabez sat at the kitchen table and realised just how lucky he was. He knew there was no future in wallowing in grief for his long-lost friend and that Sam wouldn't have wanted him to. He could well imagine his mate saying, "Pull yoursen together, Gittins."

Chapter 14

After work on a wet Thursday, Alan popped in early doors to the pub opposite the newspaper office. It had been a hard day and he felt the need to unwind with a swift pint. Considering it was just 6pm, the Mason's was busy.

Waiting to be served, Alan looked through into the bar and saw Clive and Wacker. He went through to join them.

"What are you having, Al?" said Wacker.

"No, I'll get my own."

"Be like that then!"

"I've got the car," said Alan, "so I can only have a quicky."

"Did you hear about Terry getting the bullet from the supermarket?" said Clive.

"No, what for?"

"Well apparently he'd got a piece of wood off an old pallet, they leaned the rest of the pallet against the wall as a wicket and his mate was bowling cabbages at him. Terry was in the process of knocking one for six when one of the bosses walked in. 'What the bloody hell's going on here?' Terry bawls back, 'Piss off! I'm 36 not out.' Both Terry and the bowler were dismissed halfway through the first innings. Terry asked me if I thought he could do them for unfair dismissal. What's more, he wasn't joking!"

They descended into hysterical laughter.

When the giggling had subsided, Alan said, "Changing the subject, look at these…"

From his camera case he took out the photographs he had taken of the house. Both his friends asked, "Who's the soldier?"

"Buggered if I know," Alan replied. "Strange thing is, he and his dog weren't on the negative, but when I developed them there they were. Not exactly pin-sharp but they are there."

Wacker's immediate response was, "Bullshit, that's not possible."

Alan produced from his camera case the negative in question. In turn his friends both lifted it to the light and carefully inspected it.

"You must have another negative," Wacker suggested.

"No, this is definitely the one. Honest!"

"I don't know how that could happen," said Clive, "it's just not possible."

"Nor me," said Alan, "but there it is, I canner make head nor tail of it."

Over dinner that night, Alan related the story of Terry's dismissal. Donna howled with laughter even though she didn't quite get the cricket bit. On a night out with a group of friends in the pub who were telling the story of a woman called Daphne going to Lourdes, much to her embarrassment, Donna had exclaimed, "Well you do surprise me, I wouldn't have thought Daphne was the type to be interested in cricket."

On the following Sunday, Alan rang Jabez, suggesting meeting at the Cross Guns. Alan wanted him to see the photograph with the mysterious image. As he was about to leave Donna said, "Don't be late for dinner, are you taking Spey?"

"Yes, and I won't be late," he replied.

As always, when he arrived in the bar of the Cross Guns, Bert and Digger were in their usual window seat. Looking out through the front window, Alan could see Jabez's pick-up coming down the road. At the bar he ordered two pints of Shires.

"One's for Jabez is it?" Doreen asked, "He likes a handle yer know."

With two pints, Alan crossed the bar and joined Digger and Bert.

Spey followed tentatively, eyeing Dinky, who was under Bert's seat. Spey soon followed suit and got under the seat opposite where he could keep an eye on the smaller dog.

"Alright lads," Alan said.

Bert replied, "Ah, canner complain. Alright, Jabez."

"Jabez, yours is here mate." Alan slid the pint towards him across the table.

He couldn't wait to show his photograph and took it out of the large envelope, saying, "What do you make of that?" as he handed it to Jabez.

"Well that's your house," Jabez said, "and although it's fuzzy that's Sam and Patch on the left, where'd you get that from?"

"I took it," Alan announced.

"Not possible," Jabez replied, "you'd have only been a nipper then."

Alan responded, saying, "You don't understand. I took that photo a few weeks back."

"I've heard about what you can do," Bert joined in, "Yule a clever bugger and no mistake, it's funny though, the section where Sam is looks out of focus, fuzzy - almost ghostlike."

Defensively Alan said, "I anner... I haven't," correcting himself, "done anything to them. This is straight from the negative, honest!"

Digger took some glasses out of a battered case. They were greasy, scratched and held together with adhesive tape. "Let's have a look."

Bert said, "It's a wonder you can see anything through those."

Digger, slightly aggressively, said, "I can see, I can see as well as any bugger."

He peered at the photo close up and then stretched his arms as far as he could reach and confirmed the others' findings. "Oh ah, that's him alright, that's Sam, so come on, how did you do it?"

"It is a straightforward photo," Alan insisted.

"Pull the other bugger, it's got bells on."

"No honest, I'll show you the negative," then he thought better of it, because they would see there were no figures on it and definitely think it was a leg-pull.

So he changed the subject, put away the photo, and addressed Jabez. "How do you fancy a bit of lake fishing next Thursday? I can skive off for the day."

"Magic, that'll suit me down to the ground," Jabez replied enthusiastically. "It's my turn to drive, pick you up at 8am."

"Great," said Alan, "although I don't know too much about stillwater fishing."

Bert butted in, "You never get me a bit of trout."

"I thought you didn't like trout?" said Jabez.

"Well I do if it's free."

Digger butted in, "Well me, I love trout."

"I'll see if I can get you one on Thursday, pay you back for all those veggies." Alan said.

"Oh give over mon," said Digger.

Chapter 15

On arriving at the lake, which was one thousand feet or so up in the Welsh mountains, Alan carried the outboard down to the boat which was hired for the day from Mrs Morgan at the village café.

Jabez carried the large leisure battery that would power the boat down the rickety jetty. Rods, oars and tackle boxes followed. It was a perfect day; a mixture of cloud and sun and a nice ripple running down the lake.

They fished hard all morning without touching a fish.

"Strange isn't it," said Alan, "when I fish from the bank, I try to cast out as far out as I can, but when I'm in a boat I fish towards the bank. Shall we stop for lunch?"

Alan lifted the outboard and as they approached the shore they pulled the boat up onto a sandy beach to eat their sandwiches. Overhead, two young buzzards were harrying a red kite which was hanging in the wind above the hill opposite.

Patchy weather and a change of flies saw both men take fish in quick succession after lunch. The first fell to Jabez who grunted, "Yes!"

As Jabez was playing his fish, Alan felt a solid take on his line.

Jabez netted his own fish and then Alan's. Another two fish each were in the boat, all lovely overwintered rainbows, full-finned and shiny silver.

On these trips Jabez would often reveal some details about his old friend. Consequently, little by little, Alan felt he was getting to know Sam.

The battery was beginning to lose power and the wind sent a shudder of impending rain down the lake. Jabez echoed Alan's feelings, "Shall we call it a day?"

At the jetty they unloaded the battery, outboard and oars. Once again, Jabez carried the battery and Alan the outboard. The boat was locked at its mooring and the oars pushed into the security of the lockable metal tube. Rods were taken down, fish placed in bags and wellingtons swapped for shoes.

It was late after the drive from Wales so they headed straight for the Cross Guns for a quick pint. In the pub there was only Bert sitting at the bar, chatting to Doreen.

"No Digger?" asked Alan.

"There he is," said Bert.

They looked out of the window to see Digger pushing his old bike down through the village.

"He never rides his bike," Bert commented, "I think he just uses it to keep himself upright when he's had one too many."

When Digger entered, Alan pointed to the plastic bag on the end of the bar. "That's your fish, Digger."

Jabez handed his over, "And here's yours, Bert."

Doreen chipped in, "So where's mine then?"

Jabez replied, "I've got a big one for you."

"And the trout's a big'un an' all," Bert quipped.

Doreen scolded him, "Grimshaw, your mind's like a sewer."

Jabez looked a little embarrassed at being the butt of Bert's risqué humour.

During the early days of that summer the sun shone for two weeks solid and the barbecue was in constant use. Alan had invested in a gas version and since then was a complete convert. He liked it because it was instant and when the fat dropped onto the baffle plate it ignited, recycling the flavours.

For Billy and Molly, *al fresco* living became an adventure which they loved. They erected a tent in the garden with two plastic chairs and a table which gave them a sense of independence. They often slept in the tent, and being near enough to the house should the unexpected happen, Donna and Alan had no objections to this. Also, Spey slept between the children, keeping a watchful eye on them.

On such a night, a breeze got up, rustling the tent and shivering the trees. Clouds skittered across the moon and an owl hooted. Not too far away, a dog barked, waking Molly and inducing a soft growl from Spey. She reached over, prodding Billy, but he was fast asleep in his sleeping bag with his head covered.

"Did you hear that?" she whispered.

"What?" he said.

"That dog barking," she shivered.

He turned over, saying, "Go to sleep."

Molly lay there in the darkness, listening to the noises of the night. From the darkness came the sound of someone moving about in their garden and again a dog barking. Spey growled.

Molly found the torch at the back of the tent and aimed it at Billy.

"What now?" he grumbled.

"There is someone out there."

"Go to sleep, you're a bloody nutter."

She responded by getting out of her sleeping bag, taking the torch and going back into the house with Spey following her into the hallway. Before she could go upstairs, Billy came through the door.

Molly blurted out, "What are you doing?"

"Well," he replied, "I don't like being there on my own."

"You are just a scaredy cat, Billy Tait."

At the top of the stairs, Alan appeared in his dressing gown. "What's all this noise about?"

Molly got in first, "There was someone out there in our garden."

Alan descended the stairs and reached up to the right of the door, switching on the floodlight which lit up the garden. He opened the door and looked around. He did think he saw a shadowy figure through the rose trellis and he was sure he heard the faint bark of a dog. He shut the door, not wanting to alarm the children. "Nothing there, now go to bed and let's get some sleep."

They argued their way up the stairs, Billy saying, "See, I told you so! You must have been dreaming, you nutter."

Alan dropped his dressing gown to the floor and slipped back into bed next to Donna. He lay there for a while, thinking. *Has this got anything to do with Sam and Patch?* He cuddled up to Donna's back, pulled the duvet up and drifted into a dreamy half-sleep. In graphic detail he dreamed of Jabez, Sam and Bert side by side, against an explosive background of shelling, the nightmare noises of war, shells raining in the darkness. Alan blinked awake in a cold sweat, as if he had been there in Northern France with them.

Donna put her hand on his shoulder. "Are you alright, darling? You were twitching and mumbling all night."

"Yes," he replied, "just a bad dream, I shouldn't have had that cheese butty for supper."

At work the following Wednesday, Alan had a call from Clive, reminding him it was Terry's birthday and some of the lads were meeting at the King's Arms that night.

"Sounds good to me," he said, "I'll see you there."

On his arrival home, Alan said, "Do you mind if I go for a pint with the boys, darling?"

"Why do you only call me darling when you want something? Of course I don't mind. Is that the village old boys from the Cross Guns or Terry, Clive and that lot?"

"The latter," he replied, "it's Terry's birthday. I won't be late, I'll make sure I get the last bus."

When Alan arrived at the King's Arms, Jackie said, "Your lot are in the lounge, there's one in for you, Terry ordered the round at bar prices and then went into the lounge. Crafty little bugger, that one."

The gang were sitting at a large oval table. "Cheers," Alan greeted them. "Happy Birthday, Tel."

After a couple of pints the same old subjects arose. As ever, they began reminiscing over old times. They had been mates since they were children and still kept in contact on a fairly regular basis, although some of them had drifted away, one having emigrated to Canada to join his father and Alan's old fishing partner Stevo spending most of his time at Her Majesty's Pleasure.

Terry updated the lads, "Stevo was caught bang to rights breaking into a factory. Apparently they caught him coming through a window."

Alan was getting the third round of drinks as the lounge door opened and two young women entered, the second being Emily Longhurst. Seeing Alan at the bar she went straight over to him.

"Hi Mr Tait." She oozed youthful, enthusiastic sexuality and Alan found himself colouring slightly. She continued, "This is my friend, Dandy."

When Alan returned to the table his mates all asked in chorus, "Who is *she*?"

"Just a girl from the office," he muttered.

"You sly old dog, what's her name?" Terry asked.

"Emily Longhurst," Alan replied.

"What a stunner, should be called Emily Longlegs."

"Shurrup Terry, she'll hear you!" Alan chided.

At 9am next morning, Alan bumped into Emily in the corridor.

"Excuse me Mr Tait, I wonder if you could help me?"

"Do my best," he replied.

"I want to write a feature on the D-Day landings for the anniversary and I need a photographer. Also, I want to interview people who were actually there and get some photographs, hopefully when they were young soldiers and how they are today. Any ideas?"

"I can do better than that. I have a couple of friends who were there, so leave it a few days and I'll arrange a meeting. In the meantime I'll ask them if they have any old photos and I'll take their portraits."

"That would be ace," she replied, "Thanks Mr Tait."

"You can call me Alan you know, Mr Tait makes me feel old," was Alan's parting remark.

"OK, that's brill Alan," she said enthusiastically.

I must get 'Longlegs' out of my head or there will be a time when I call her by that name and she'll take me for a pervert, Alan thought.

At close of play that day, Alan stopped off at Jabez's smallholding. He parked on the grass verge, opened the gate and walked down the drive. The sheepdog came up the drive barking and then, recognising Alan, wagged his tail and lay down, inviting Alan to stoop and stroke him.

Alan explained to Jabez about the D-Day feature

98

that Emily was planning and asked if the two of them could come and interview him. The response was a positive yes, Jabez would be only too pleased.

Chapter 16

Alan left the office with Emily in her Mini. As she drove across town, Alan tried to avert his gaze from her legs. He tried to keep on the subject of work, "I'll take the photographs after you have done your interview, I don't want him getting camera shy."

At the smallholding, Alan opened the gate while Emily drove through and parked on the drive. The collie came up to greet them, low to the ground with its tail raising dust as he neared them.

"Is he friendly?" Emily asked, "You never know with collies."

"Oh he's fine," Alan responded.

Emily proffered the back of her hand to the dog and was soon stroking him.

Laura answered the front door and Alan introduced Emily.

"Come through my dear, would you like a cup of tea?" asked Laura.

"Where's Jabez?" Alan asked.

"I'll give him a shout, he's in the bathroom beautifying himself for the photos, acting like he's some sort of filmstar, he is."

When the tea arrived it was on a tray with two cups, a teapot, sugar with a doily protecting it and two plates with scones.

"Thought you could manage a scone with your tea, my lovelies," said Laura.

The room was full of old-fashioned, ageless charm and smelled of furniture polish. Its heartbeat was the mantel clock, which had ticked through history and added a soothing quality. Emily and Alan were sipping their tea when the door opened and there stood Jabez.

Alan hardly recognised his friend. Jabez's hair had been swept to one side in a rakish manner and his face shone. He wore a well-ironed white shirt and something else Alan hadn't seen before. Around his neck was his regimental tie.

Alan gasped, "You look a million dollars, Jabez!"

Jabez responded with a good-natured, "Are you taken the proverbial out of me?"

"No, no, never let it be said. This is Emily, our reporter who's doing the feature."

The clean-shaven face of Jabez lit up when he saw Emily, for although he knew he was past his sell-by date, he still had an eye for the ladies.

Alan said, "I'll leave you two to it then, it's much easier one-to-one, you can talk more freely without an audience."

They sat either side of the polished dining table and Jabez opened up as he recalled his experiences of those memorable days of June 1944.

Meanwhile, Alan sat with Laura in the kitchen and watched her work.

"Lovely looking girl, that reporter of yours," she commented.

"Is she?" said Alan defensively.

"Yes, Jabez will love that interview." Laura continued, "He appreciates the finer things in life, you know."

The lounge door remained shut for well over an hour. When they emerged, Emily enthused, "I've got some great stuff. He's a very interesting man, your husband."

Alan suggested the photographs would be better taken outside, "Natural light is always better."

He shot two rolls of film; the light was perfect and Jabez an obliging model.

"You're a right poser you are, Jabez," Alan said. "I'll let you have a look at them before we publish, so you can kick out any you don't like. We'll push off now, thanks for the tea and scones, Mrs G."

Emily added, "Yes thank you very much, the scones were fab."

She drove Alan back to the office and as he got out of the car she said, "Thanks for that, Alan, what a lovely man. Hard to imagine him going through the horrors of D-Day. See you in the office tomorrow."

"Yes!" he replied, "All things being equal."

Having used the phrase he thought to himself, *What does that actually mean?*

On the way home, Alan called in at the Cross Guns. Only Digger and Bert were in the bar. Doreen came up from cellar saying, "Sorry to have kept you waiting."

"No problem," Alan said, "I've only just come through the door."

"The usual," she presumed, already pulling a pint of Shires.

"Lovely, thanks," he said as he walked over to the window seats.

Sitting down he said, "OK lads, cheers. Bert, are you in tomorrow night about six?"

"Where else, but why?"

"The paper's doing a feature on the D-Day landings.

"And don't tell me," said Bert, "you want some pictures of a real life hero."

"I'll have a young lady reporter with me," warned Alan, "so you'll have to watch your language."

"Ah dunner you worry, mon," Bert assured him.

As Alan left, he turned, saying, "Don't forget, six o'clock. See you tomorrow - oh yes and and no need to dress up, I want you to look normal."

"He'll never be that," quipped Doreen from behind the bar.

"Alright, alright," said Bert, "What's this - a bash Bert night?"

The following evening, Emily Longhurst's Mini was parked outside the Cross Guns when Alan arrived on foot. Emily was reading the evening paper when he tapped on the car window. She jumped, then opened the door. "Evening Alan, have you walked?"

"Yes, it's not far. I often walk down so I can enjoy a couple of jars," he replied.

Once inside, Alan introduced Bert and Digger. "This is Emily Longhurst."

Bert's eyes lit up when he saw Emily.

Digger's hat nearly fell off, he stammered and coloured up like a besotted schoolboy.

"Were you both in the war?" she enquired while Alan was getting a round of drinks.

"No, just me," Bert said proudly. "Digger was keeping the home fires burning and supplied vegetables for half the village."

Digger added, "And in the Home Guard, I was an' all."

Alan suggested the interview should take place in the lounge as it offered privacy and was empty. Just over an hour later, Bert and Emily emerged smiling and both looking well pleased with themselves, as though they had been friends for years.

"Thanks for that, Mr Grimshaw, it was fascinating and just what I needed."

"You can call me Bert, everyone in the village does, even the kids."

"Can I buy you a drink?" she offered.

He smiled, "Ah, if you twist me arm."

The four of them sat together and Bert was the first

to speak. "One of the village lads bought it during the first landing and RSM Sam Leftwich a few days later. He was a good mate of mine an' all, near broke my heart it did. He lived in Alan's house you know, up at The Stables."

"Oh, we could give him a mention in the feature," Emily enthused.

"Yes, I think Mary, his widow, would like that. Jabez and his missus keep in touch with her."

Dinky appeared from under Bert's seat and, catlike, rubbed himself against Longlegs. Like his human counterparts, he appeared to appreciate a fine pair of legs.

She leaned forward and stroked the little terrier, "What a gorgeous little dog, how do I contact Mrs Leftwich?"

"I'll sort that out for you, Emily, leave it to me," said Alan.

It was duly arranged that Jabez would bring Mary to their house the following Sunday. When that day arrived, Mary Leftwich sat between Jabez and Laura, Emily's Mini following them up the drive.

Donna greeted them as they walked up to the front door and Billy shot out, "Going fishing, Mr Gittins?"

Donna commanded, "Go and shout your dad his visitors are here, he's cutting grass behind the greenhouse."

As soon as Donna saw Mary, she recognised her from the photograph, even though at least 30 years had elapsed. Mary's silvering hair was neatly tied up with a pearl-headed pin holding it in place. Although time and sadness had taken their toll, she stood erect and her beauty was still very much in evidence. Her pale blue eyes still carried a twinkle.

Donna shook hands with Mary, saying, "Make yourself at home; but of course this was your home, sorry."

Alan said, "Donna, this is Emily. She's writing the article I told you about."

Emily said hello to Donna then turned to Mary, "I thought we could just walk around the house and gardens and talk. I have a recording machine and I'll base my writing on that information. Naturally I'll let you see what I have written before it's published."

Jabez, Laura, Donna and Alan sat on garden chairs and Molly said, "Can I go with the pretty ladies?"

"No, you sit still and let them get on with their work," Donna commanded.

As they walked Mary said, "I was so happy here with my Sam, everything was perfect until the war came along. Oh, how I hated that war, it ruined everything for me."

Emily put her arm around the older woman who said, "I'm alright dear."

A single tear trickled down Mary's cheek.

"Do you want to stop now?" Emily suggested.

"No, no I want to get it out of my system."

At the end of the garden they sat on an ancient bench, the sort you might find in a public park. "Sam bought this, I'm glad to see it is still here and well looked after. Sam always said he would come back and, sitting here, I can sort of feel his presence. I know that may sound a bit daft, but that's how I feel, and we did spend many happy hours here, just talking or sometimes just sitting, enjoying the silence."

They sat there and talked. The day was warm and Mary related the past in soft, well-educated tones. Emily was overcome with feelings of affection for her. This was a love story and all Emily could do was constantly check that the recorder was operating, and listen.

Mary enthused over their many picnics and she told of their dog, Patch. "He was Sam's soulmate and a comfort to me. Cruelly, he was shot around the same time as Sam was killed in France. We never found out who killed him, but everyone pointed the finger at Hooky, a local recluse who was and still is universally disliked. By the way," she added, "I have a few photographs in the pick-up which you may find useful."

Emily said, "Super, shall we join the others? I've got plenty of stuff for my article."

They walked across the large expanse of lawn and could hear the others were in full conversation.

"Everything okay with you two? I expect you could drink a cup of tea."

Emily responded, "I could murder one, Mrs Tait."

After her tea Emily said, "I'd better make tracks. I'm lunching with Mummy and she insists on punctuality."

Mary interrupted, "Don't forget I have some photos in the pick up."

Alan volunteered, "I'll bring those into the office on Monday, promise."

They watched Emily walk to her Mini.

Mary observed, "What a gorgeous girl, so bright and caring."

Donna whispered to Alan, "She is gorgeous, isn't she?"

He, feigning disinterest, asked, "Is she? Hadn't really noticed."

"Lovely legs as well," she added.

"Can't say I ever looked," he lied.

In time, Jabez suggested, "I think we had better get Mary home."

She agreed, "Yes, it's getting late and we don't want to abuse your kind hospitality."

"Nonsense," Donna said, "you are always welcome here, come any time, I'll be glad of the company."

"Thank you. I do feel happy here and I feel closer to Sam. Strange; I suppose it was because we were so blissfully happy here until the war spoiled everything."

Molly looked wistfully at the old woman and then blurted out, "We've seen a soldier and a dog looking at the house, honest."

Donna quickly joined in, saying, "Mary doesn't want to hear your silly ramblings."

"Well we did, and Dad did as well."

Billy adopted his usual stance, "You're off your trolley, you are."

Mary gave Molly a knowing, wistful smile, but remained silent.

However, fearing the talk would upset the old lady, Donna said, "That's enough, Molly."

The subject was dropped.

When the feature appeared it was very well received. Bert took his copy and posted it on the wall of the pub.

"See, that's me and Jabez. Heroes we were, it's here in black and white."

When the paper arrived at the Gittins' smallholding, Jabez took his copy into the lounge and spread it out on the polished oak table, borrowing Laura's reading glasses so as to get a proper look at the piece.

There was a photograph of all the lads shortly after war broke out, at battalion training camp on Salisbury Plain. There was a grinning Bert, casually lying down with his hand propping up his head, on which his beret was perched at a jaunty angle. Jabez scanned the photograph. There he was in the background with his arm around Sam Leftwich. He felt a tide of emotion rising up in him. It seemed only yesterday that they had sat off the coast of France, looking at the dark silhouette of the Brittany coastline; a nervous fleet prior to the impending attack.

He remembered it was a moonlit night. He remembered the cold feeling of fear. He remembered Operation Neptune and the great armada of ships on either side of them.

He remembered the faces of the young soldiers; pale, rabbit-like and sickly scared, and he remembered looking at Sam, who as always conveyed an aura of confidence.

"Do you want a cup of tea, darling?" Laura offered, breaking him out of his daydream. "Are you alright? You look like you have seen a ghost."

She could see he was upset, she had seen that look before.

"Yes that'd be lovely," he said, "then I'd better get on with a bit of work."

Chapter 17

After he had fed the pigs, Jabez sat in his old seat and in a half-sleep drifted back to 1944 with the war still in full swing. He and the rest of the men had been given embarkation leave. They all had the feeling something big was about to happen; troops of many nations were mobilising, convoys of khaki-camouflaged military vehicles and heavy stuff were apparent across the country.

Sam and Mary took advantage of their short leave together and with Patch they drove into the countryside and set up a picnic by a favourite small brook, no wider than a step but still carrying a strong, gurgling current. Patch retrieved stones even when they were underwater and Sam and Mary, barefoot, dangled their toes in the icy bubbles.

The war seemed a million miles away and Sam shoved it firmly into the back of his mind. He pumped and lit his Primus stove, dipped the kettle into the stream, and very soon steam was hissing from its short spout.

"Tea always tastes better out of doors," Sam observed as he ate his favourite - egg and cress sandwiches.

He and Mary sat on the soft sheep-shorn grass as they sipped their tea, ate their sandwiches and contemplated what the next few months would bring. At that precise moment, Sam felt supremely happy, as did Mary, as did Patch, who had settled on the corner of the tartan rug and blinked in a sunny slumber.

The leave passed all too quickly and soon they were preparing for the parting. Sam had worked out a

109

crude sort of code so that Mary would at least know where he was, without upsetting the censors. 'Is uncle's foot any better?' meant they were in France, 'How's the dog?' meant Italy and 'Has auntie been back?' meant North Africa. They had been using this method all through the war, however on this occasion they had a good idea the target was France and an assault on mainland Europe.

Their last night together was sleepless and they held onto each other to the point of near-suffocation. Their bodies were as one and each worried for the other as the time got nearer to their parting. All too soon, morning blasted through the curtains, causing their rude awakening and the cold reality of dawn and what lay ahead.

Sam's kitbag was leaning against the newel post in the hallway, ready for the off, as the two of them sat looking at each other and eating a full English breakfast.

Afterwards, they walked down the drive, hand-in-hand with Patch between them. When they reached the road, Sam said, "You go back now."

The dog was intent on going with Sam, so Mary put him on his lead. She kissed her husband and a tell-tale tear ran down her pallid cheek.

"I'm sorry, I was determined not to cry."

He comforted her, "Don't be unhappy, I will return, whatever happens. That's a promise, and we'll have lots more picnics."

She watched him walk down the road towards the village and, heeding that old fable that you should never watch the one you love go out of sight, she turned away and walked back towards the house. Once indoors the sadness welled up in her aching throat and she sobbed uncontrollably. She tasted salty tears and wondered how was she going to manage without her beloved Sam. He was her strength and rock.

Bert and young Gareth Davies were waiting outside the Cross Guns when Sam arrived, Gareth surrounded by his mum and dad, aunts and uncles. He looked like a little boy, too young to be going to war, thought Sam. He'd been delivering papers just a couple of years ago.

"Morning Sam," Bert greeted him.

Gareth's mum called out to Sam, "You will look after him won't you, Mr Leftwich? He's my baby."

Gareth spluttered, "Oh Mum."

She kissed him, saying, "Have you got a clean hankie?"

His embarrassment prompted him to be the first to move off, kitbag slung over his shoulder.

The three of them marched to the top of the village where the lorry was to pick them up. Some of the older men clapped, shouting, "Good luck boys, give 'em hell!"

One or two of them had tears of guilt in their eyes.

Two small boys sat on the wall of the railway bridge and shouted, "Go and get him, Mr Grimshaw, give them Germans a bloody good hiding, Mr Leftwich!"

Another shouted, "Give Adolf one up the bracket!"

The whole country was alive with troops. The lorry stopped outside Jabez Gittins' house. He came up the drive fully kitted and ready to go. His wife Laura stood at the door, sadly waving but putting on a confident, brave face. Underneath she was frightened and wondered if she would ever see her husband again.

Sam reached out a hand to help Jabez into the back of the truck, smiling and wishing him a good morning.

When assembled at the barracks, they were inspected as they stood in expectant lines, hoping that they would soon find out their fate. When they marched through the town towards the railway station, people lined the streets, clapping and shouting encouragement.

The troop train, hissing and billowing steam, chugged into Platform Four. It was crammed full of noisy soldiers. There was as much smoke inside as there was out, thanks to all the cigarettes being nervously and excitedly puffed on. They jostled to find seats while manhandling their kitbags. Some of them ate sandwiches that mothers, wives and girlfriends had insisting on making them.

On arrival at the docks it was obvious that it was indeed something momentous which was about to happen as the whole place was buzzing. Heavy equipment had been loaded onto numerous ships. The dockside was filled with soldiers of several nations being organised with verbal assaults from sergeants and corporals who were trying to retain a semblance of order.

Bert, Sam, Jabez and Gareth, once onboard, found bunks in the dank bowels of the ship.

"It pongs a bit down here dunner it?" Bert commented.

A great armada, thousands of ships, was assembled as part of Operation Neptune, ready for the assault on the French coast.

Eighteen-year-old Gareth drew some comfort from being a part of such a massive force and in being in the company of locals Bert, Sam and Jabez, but fear of the unknown was always at the back of his mind. To the left and right there was the huge Neptune armada, pregnant with landforces ready to spill their lethal contents onto the French soil as part of Operation Overlord.

Sam had full confidence his men were trained up into a well oiled fighting unit.

From the deck they could see the Normandy coastline like a cardboard cut-out, silhouetted by the moonlight and peeking through heavy cumulus clouds. In the distance a plane went down like a shooting star, followed by a massive explosive flare on impact, followed by a dark plume of smoke.

"I'm bursting for a piss!" cried young Gareth.

Bert advised, "Dunner worry about that mon, you'll soon wash it off when we hit the beach, you can piss in the sea."

There were plenty of white, scared faces caught in the moonlight. They looked at each other, seeking reassurance.

Sam instructed, "Don't forget - when you are on the beach, keep moving. Don't stop for anyone, even friends, the medics will see to casualties."

As they neared the beach, the shore batteries opened up, great explosive cascades of water flew into the air. Further in, the rattle of machine gun fire signalled what was waiting for them and a shiver passed through the landing craft.

When the front dropped down at the water's edge, they all scrambled out, screaming and running up the beach, looking for cover. The water was over three feet deep, which slowed their progress. There were lots of casualties strewn all across the shore and more drifting like flotsam in the shallows, turning the sea a sad, sad red.

Sam, with several others including Jabez, had found temporary cover behind a huge concrete block, part of an anti-tank defence which had been split in half by the earlier Royal Navy bombardment.

Jabez asked Sam, "Have you seen Bert?"

"No, but I think he's over to the right."

Jabez scanned the area. Behind a breakwater he saw an arm raise followed by a thumbs up sign. *Yes, that's got to be Bert*, he thought.

The next goal was a solid sea wall. Sam stood up, shouting, "Come on lads!" and racing to the next lot of cover. Once behind the sea wall they were comparatively safe, although twenty yards on the other side of the wall was a pillbox.

Sam asked Bert, "Have you seen young Gareth?"

"'Fraid not, he were cut down before he even got to the water, never did get his piss, didn't even get on shore, poor little bugger."

Sam felt he had let down Gareth's family and he responded angrily. "Right, let's knock out that bloody pillbox, let's do it for Gareth. Concentrate as much covering fire on that slit as you can."

With that he pulled himself up, wriggled through the railings, and ran 25 yards. Using skills gained on the village cricket pitch, he threw a grenade side arm through the slit. He followed it with a second Mills bomb, shouting, "Come on boys, let's go get 'em."

At least a dozen gained shelter behind the pill box, from which point they could see down through the smoke, the road leading to Caen. Others had dropped into the roadside ditch, which offered a natural trench.

"Let's push on boys," came the words from Major Hamilton Whitfield. He looked through binoculars, adding, "It all looks quite clear other than that stand of trees."

There were trees either side of the road about a quarter of a mile along.

Addressing Jabez, the major said, "Take these glasses with you, Corporal, and see if you can get a better outlook on the situation up ahead."

Once installed high enough, Jabez lay in the grass. He trained the binoculars on the trees, the smell of the summer grass and a huge bumble bee landing near enough for him to study it closely, making him nostalgic for home. He moved a little further up the hill and, taking a gamble, stood up. Keeping out of sight behind a tree, he was able to make out tanks and a number of troops waiting.

He dropped quickly to the ground and scurried back, slithering down painfully on his arse to the pillbox to report his findings.

"Good work Corporal," the Major smiled, saying in a condescending manner, "Gittins isn't it?"

Jabez responded, "Yes Sir."

With Jabez's information, a prolonged mortar attack was ordered, which had the desired effect of bringing the tanks into the open and returning fire up the road towards them.

A handful of men under orders had progressed up the road in the cover of the ditch. When in position, with the aid of a bazooka aimed with great accuracy, the chain of the first tank was smashed, stopping it in its tracks and effectively blocking the road for a while.

All that day the fighting was fierce and progress up the pitted road was slow.

Originally the plan was to take the city on D-Day itself, 6th June 1944. Initially the landings on Sword Beach had apparently been a great success but although the Allies had penetrated the Atlantic Wall and pushed south, the division were unable to reach the city, which was their final objective. They were held up six kilometres away and the road to Caen was effectively blocked due to successful counter-attacks by the 21st Panzer Division.

Consequently, on 9th June, Caen was still firmly in German hands.

Progress was slow, measured in yards rather than miles, and expensive in terms of lives and equipment. It was down to the fortitude of individual men, operating in groups that inched towards success; men who were unaware of the total picture of Overlord and just concentrated on playing their part.

Eventually the advance found Sam, Bert and Jabez on the outskirts of Caen, or what remained of it. There was little left standing, buildings had been flattened by the bombardment of the Allies and the city smouldered.

Sam guided his men into a wrecked smallholding for shelter. Darkness fell so that many fires could be seen. He said, "Put that corrugated sheet against the window, but quietly, mind. Has anybody seen Grimshaw?"

"He was behind that flattened farmhouse last I saw him," replied Private Carswell.

Shortly, there was a scuffling outside. They all fell quiet, aiming their rifles at the direction of the sound. From beneath fallen roof beams and covered in dust, Bert materialised on hands and knees, crawling over rubble and holding two dead chickens in his right hand, a huge grin spread across his grubby face.

"Where did yow get them from?" a young ginger-haired Brummie soldier asked.

"Country secret owd lad, country secret," Bert mocked.

"Ow yow going to cook 'em?" the Brummie further enquired.

"Well now, that's no country secret, lad," said Bert, "I'm going to spit roast 'em."

In the corner of what had once been the kitchen there were smouldering roof beams and laths still just about burning. Having dressed the chicken, Bert rigged up a crude spit, using an old poker mounted on bricks. He put more roof laths onto the smouldering heap and gently blew on them. Soon the chicken fat was dropping onto the fire, making it burn more efficiently.

Jabez instructed, "Don't put too much on the fire, Grimshaw, we don't want to attract attention, we don't want Germans coming for supper."

Just as the chickens were about cooked, a young lieutenant came into the kitchen. "What's going on here?"

Bert jumped straight in, "Making a bit of supper for the boys."

With a clipped accent from beneath his clipped ginger moustache, the lieutenant addressed Sam, "Better tell your men to get some shut eye, early start tomorrow don't you know? Got sentries posted have you Sergeant? Did well today, men."

After they had torn the chickens to bits, each having a taste, the Brummie lad said, "I dow get much."

Bert, reprimanding him, said, "Ah yes but you got the parson's nose, that's the best bit, it'll put lead in your pencil, us country lads knows it's an aphrodisiac."

The Brummie replied, "What's a aphro-whatever you said?"

"You know, it makes you interested in the opposite sex," said Bert.

"Well I like women anyway, I've got a girlfriend from Acocks Green."

After their snack of chicken, some of the men fell into crumpled, exhausted heaps, falling asleep on piles of rubble.

Chapter 18

Sam tried to make himself comfortable on his rubble bed and tried to put the war and his predicament out of his mind. He imagined Mary preparing a picnic. He visualised their old hamper, every detail down to the leather strap which was hardened and cracked with age, making it difficult to buckle and unbuckle.

He could see Mary folding the gingham tablecloth, the two enamel plates and mugs, the cutlery wrapped in paper napkins. Then the sandwiches, his favourite egg and cress, cheddar cheese - just about the only cheese available during the war - with home-made pickle. Scones with farm butter and home-made strawberry jam. Then there was his contribution - his old Primus stove, teabags and sugar in screw-top jars in an old large tin. There was also Patch's bowl, and his biscuits.

That's the first thing I'm doing on my next leave. Mary, Patch and me on a picnic. Sam lay back with a smile on his face and drifted in and out of sleep, dreaming of home and anxious about what the morning would bring.

Outside it was pitch black and a semi silence fell across the battlefield, which was rudely broken by the occasional burst of machine gun fire. In the early hours a dog barking woke Sam, reminding him immediately of Patch and of home. The light was pushing back the stars and doing its best to wake the day. Soon the men were rising from the rubble, lighting up cigarettes and coughing. There were moans and groans. Stiff limbs stirred. Somebody said, "What I wouldn't give for a cup of char."

"Right men, get your gear together, we are moving out in half an hour," Sam ordered.

There was a concentrated smell of hot urine as someone had relieved themselves on last night's fire, which had been smouldering.

"Which dirty bastard pissed on the fire?"

The Brummie answered, "I did, we don't want the Krauts to see any smoke dow we?"

Someone moaned, "Yes, but they could smell that Brummie piss in Berlin, I'll be glad to get out of here."

"Come on lads, let's get a move on," Sam ordered, "big day today."

They left their cover and tentatively walked out into the early morning sun, rubbing and blinking their eyes. Ahead, the city of Caen seemed to consist of little other than piles of rubble and collapsed buildings, the smell of cordite in the air. The further they got into the city, the more cover was available and they moved from building to building, making good progress.

Suddenly, machine gun fire ripped into the ruin they were in and they quickly took cover.

Sam ordered, "Keep your heads down till we can find out what we are up against."

At this point the young lieutenant, he with the clipped ginger moustache and clipped accent, appeared and snapped, "What's the hold up here lads?"

Sam replied, "There's heavy fire coming in from that big building to the right, Sir."

"Well we'd better do something about that then hadn't we, and pretty damned quick, don't you know." He turned and marched back, not bothering to take cover.

There was a murmur from the ranks, "Bloody prat."

"That's enough, he is on our side," Sam admonished.

"Is that good or bad?" Bert joked.

"That'll do, Grimshaw."

Mortar fire was directed at the big building, sending German troops scurrying down to take cover. At this point the men, led by Sam, charged forward, firing as they went, and soon occupied the house the Germans had been holed up in. The fighting went like that all day, building to building, little by little, each piece of ground being hard fought for, dust and death everywhere.

They advanced into an avenue that led to a small square which had obviously been a market area, with an open-sided building supported by carved wooden pillars. The red tiled roof had collapsed on one side and while it was no use as a market, it provided some cover from incoming fire.

Chapter 19

In England Mary had just received a letter marked *'ACTIVE SERVICE'* and she knew it was from Sam. She couldn't wait to read it but Jesse Simpkins had called in and chatted endlessly, mostly about her daughter Madge. Mary tried to look interested but really wished she would go. However, the verbals came in torrents, none of which were registering.

Eventually Jesse said, "Well, can't stop, lots to do, this won't get the baby fed or whatever they say."

Mary walked to her usual seat at the end of the garden. She sat down, enjoying some unexpected sunny weather, and Patch jumped up on the bench next to her. Mary took the letter from inside her blouse where she had secreted it and carefully opened it. She wanted to be alone when she read it; after all, it was personal, between Sam and her.

My Darling Wife,

I thought I knew what it meant to be in love before we were married but I'm afraid my ideas fell far short of reality. I had no idea that such an intense feeling could be held by one person for another. I thank my lucky stars every time I think of you (which is all the time) and for you thinking me good enough to be your husband. On my part I feel I am not worthy of such a truth in that. Oh, how I miss you and crave for that closeness again, but even though I miss you terribly I can console myself in the knowledge that our marriage is far and away above a mere physical relationship.

It is difficult finding time to write as we seem to be continually on the move but I hope this short letter will help you cope with our parting. If you ever feel down in the dumps, think of all the good times we have had. On my part, I try to imagine I am on a picnic with you and Patch and you are always the last thing on my mind when I go to sleep and I say 'Goodnight my love'. I know that sounds soppy and sentimental but it does give me peace of mind.

Things are going well here and hopefully this mess will be successfully completed and we can all come home to our loved ones. Words cannot tell how much I love you but as this is the only medium open to me, please excuse me. Give Patch a pat for me and take care of yourself, you're so precious to me.

Your loving Husband
Sam xxxx
P.S. Is uncle's foot any better?

Mary felt an ache in her throat and tears trickled down her pale cheeks. Patch moved closer to her and rested his chin on her lap as if he understood her emotions. She stroked him and gained some comfort from his presence. The dog looked up at her and she didn't feel quite so alone.

She thought to herself, *If there's better therapy than stroking a dog, I've yet to find it.* Folding up the letter and carefully putting it back in its envelope, she beckoned to him. "Come on Patch, that's enough crying for today."

That night Mary lay in bed and as always, although not a true believer, with an aching throat she said the Lord's Prayer, adding, "And please protect my lovely Sam, and send him home to me." The sleep that followed was broken and irregular. She woke at 3am and made a cup of tea, reading Sam's letter again. She dropped it by the bed and drifted back to sleep, dreaming of Sam and praying he was safe.

Chapter 20

In Normandy it was the same start to the day as any other. Dirty and dishevelled, with days of stubble, Jabez was the first to stir as streaks of light penetrated the gaps in the walls. He stood up and stretched to get his oxygen levels up and enliven his muscles.

Gradually moans, groans and coughing filled their overnight shelter as the rest of the squad rubbed their eyes and realised their situation and their depressing predicament. The radio operator received a message from headquarters, which ordered a coordinated attack by the British and Canadian forces to kick off at 8am.

There was little left of the ancient city of Caen; mostly it had been destroyed, such a tragedy as many of the buildings dated back to the Middle Ages. Unfortunately for the city it was a key target, being a road hub and lying astride the Orme River and Caen Canal, two water obstacles that were natural defensive positions if not crossed. Caen was a key objective as it would open up the whole of Western France and was a must if the invasion was to succeed.

The men, with Sam leading from the front, moved cautiously up a narrow street. A machine gun opened up and Sam barked, "Get down!"

They ducked behind a substantial wall while they tried to assess the situation and ascertain the source of the gunfire.

After some minutes they realised that whoever was firing, it wasn't being directed at their small group. Sam said, "Let's move and take cover in that house with no roof."

It was 50 yards ahead, down a narrow alley which gave good cover. They all ran, hearts in mouths, and got to the safety of the house. Inside was what had once been someone's home; it still had family photographs on the walls and there were coffee cups on the table, indicating that the residents had made a hasty withdrawal. All the buildings had been partially or completely demolished and walls peppered by gunfire.

From this vantage point they could scan the whole of the square which lay ahead of them and with binoculars they studied each building in turn, searching for signs of life.

Sam said, "We will go round the edge of the square." He was interrupted as all of a sudden a civilian in a dusty black suit, which looked like it had been fashioned from an ancient tome, appeared through the back door. He was thin, drawn and dusty, his collarless white shirt looked like it hadn't seen water in ages. He gabbled away in French at speed, pointing to the church at the bottom of the square on the extreme left. From Sam's limited grasp of the language he gathered the man was warning them that there were several panzers hidden directly behind the church. Then the man vanished through the same door through which he had entered.

Jabez queried, "Do think we can trust him?"

"We've got nothing to lose either way," said Sam, "and he's got nothing to gain."

Co-ordinates were radioed back to base, and Sam said, "Keep your heads down and we'll see what the artillery can do."

After half an hour, the first shell whistled overhead and took the spire clean off the church. The barrage that followed ended with some spectacular starburst explosions and palls of smoke rising to the heavens from behind the church.

"Let's move it, lads," Sam ordered and they left their cover, skirting the square and using what cover they could find en route. They ran in and out of doorways and not a shot was fired. At the far side of the square they bundled into what had once been a shop. From the couple of bolts of material and some scissors left on a workbench, the consensus of opinion was that it had been a draper's. Through the front door there was a cobbled lane, with an open area to the right. There were still curtains on the front window and they peeped through them.

"I don't like that big building up to the right," Jabez observed, "ideal for a sniper."

"We've got to go anyway," Sam said, "I'll go first, train your rifles on that building, each pick a window, and keep your eyes open."

The door was opened quietly and Sam walked in a stooped position onto the pavement. There was a loud *Crack!* and Sam folded and dropped to the floor.

Jabez, without thinking, shouted, "Cover me!" He ran out, grabbing Sam's legs and pulling him behind an old stone horse trough. There he lay with his friend and he could see the sniper had done a good job.

He shouted, "I need to get him back inside."

Bert said, "Try and draw the sniper's fire and we'll nail the fucking bastard."

Jabez shouted, "Are you ready?"

Bert shouted "Yeah, we've got Marksman Carswell here, he's a crack shot, he's got the badge to prove it."

Jabez removed Sam's helmet and put it on the end of his rifle, poking it just over the edge of the horse trough. Again, the report of the gun. The helmet was sent to the ground.

"Got him, he's on the third floor, second window from the right!" Bert enthused. "Pop the helmet up again, we'll have the bastard this time."

Jabez followed the same procedure and this time

there were two shots fired. The first hit Sam's helmet and the other found its target. The sniper slumped forward and he and his rifle clattered noisily to the street.

They all shouted, "Bloody great shot, Carswell!"

Jabez pushed the front door open and carried his mate into the shop. They unravelled the bolts of cloth and spread them on the bench, carefully lying Sam on them. There was a lot of blood staining the cloth and things looked pretty bad. The men stood around him. Someone said, "We've got to stem the bleeding, I canner do it."

"I'll go and find a medic." Bert ran from the room.

Jabez got up onto the bench beside Sam and rested his friend's head in his lap. He tried to stop the bleeding by applying pressure with a handkerchief. This was clearly inefficient but at least Jabez felt he was doing something, although a great fear inhabited his body. Soon his trousers were wet with his friend's blood. The other men around the pair could see Sam was not long for this world. Jabez could feel that life was dribbling from his friend and a feeling of helplessness overwhelmed him.

Sam's eyes flickered and in a weakened voice that was barely audible he whispered, "Goodbye old mate, I'm going home to Mary."

Tears washed rivulets through the grime on Jabez's face as Sam's head flopped to one side and he was gone.

Bert, complete with medic, came through the back door saying triumphantly, "I've got one."

"Too late Bert, he's gone."

A dark cloud of despondency settled over the men, not least over Jabez and Bert, who were both devastated. Jabez went into Sam's pocket and removed his wallet and its contents to ensure they were delivered into Mary's hands. The medic removed Sam's identity disc and said, "I'll see to your mate, boys." He covered Sam up with some of the drapery.

Burying his feelings Jabez said, "Come on lads, there's a war to be won, let's do it for Sam."

Those last four words triggered a positive reaction and they echoed his words, "Let's do it for Sam." It was to become their own personal battle cry.

The rest of that day and into the evening they progressed well, through streets and alleyways, over and around walls, until they reached another property with the ground floor still intact.

"Alright lads, this will do us till morning," Jabez cried.

Once inside he went into a dark corner of the room and by torchlight read Sam's letter. He knew it would be personal and wondered if he was intruding but Sam was like a brother to him and he felt neither Sam nor Mary would object.

There were just two sheets of notepaper but only a side and a half had been written on.

My Darling Mary,

It seems an age since we were last together and being away from you doesn't get any easier. My every waking thought is of you and I try to imagine what you would be doing at any given time, wishing I could be with you and feel your closeness. Having said that I do imagine you are with me like a guardian angel and gain some comfort in this way. My body yearns to hold you, so tight that we become as one. I think the war is going well from what we know so hopefully it won't be too long before we are all together again. Jabez is proving a real Godsend, what a soldier and what a friend to have. He is a real stalwart and I am fortunate to have him with me. Bert is his usual self, cheeky little bugger, but he does help keep the men's spirits up. He cooked a chicken he'd scrounged from God knows where, plucked it and it was very

The letter stopped at this point. Jabez folded it up and felt extreme sadness, yet pride at Sam's appreciation of him.

That night he drifted in and out of sleep, dreaming he was fishing with his friend then watching him hit a six over the village cricket pavilion. When he awoke next morning it dawned on Bert that his friend was no longer with him and that his dreams were just that. He kept seeing Sam's face as the life drained out of it but he tried to concentrate on the good times they'd had.

Chapter 21

Back home at The Stables, Mary was picking the first crop of runner beans, one of Sam's favourites, when she felt a sudden cold foreboding invade her mind; an intense feeling of loneliness. She craved her husband's presence. Patch was nowhere to be seen, probably chasing rabbits, and she called him several times without success.

As she walked back to the house, a farm vehicle drew up in front. The driver got out, it was young Charlie Wilkins, the farmer from over the hill.

"Morning Mrs Leftwich. I'm not sure, but I think I have bad news for you."

Panic enveloped her. Was it Sam?

"I think this may be your dog, he's been shot."

In the back of the truck, laid out on a blood-stained potato sack, was Patch. Mary picked up his limp body, kissed his head and wept. "Where did you find him, who shot him?"

"It wunner me Missus, I found him down by the two pools, twelve-bore by the look of it."

"Well thank you for bringing him home, I appreciate it."

"No trouble, is there anything else I can do for you?"

She shook her head. Sam would be devastated, losing his soulmate. She felt an anger which was alien to her nature. *If I could find out who shot him, I'd strangle him,* she thought. Mary laid the dog on the lawn, went into the house and came out with the blanket from his basket. She kissed Patch and placed him on it with a half-chewed tennis ball, a rubber bone and his lead, and wrapped him up tightly. All this whilst sobbing, 'Oh Patch, oh Patch,' as she lifted him into their wheelbarrow. Carrying a spade, she took him down to the wood and buried him.

In the evening she thought, *I have to write to Sam, I can't not tell him, but oh my God what's it going to do to him?*

The next morning she sat at the kitchen table and made several attempts at breaking the news to her husband, but each time she screwed the paper up. She rested her elbows on the table and, head in hands, let her tears run like the rain on the window. Eventually she dried her eyes and, to clear her head, took the washing out into the garden and began pegging it out on the line. She stopped abruptly as a telegram boy on a red bicycle rode up the drive, ringing his bell to announce his arrival.

Mary felt a hollowness in her stomach. Fear shook her and her legs felt like jelly, about to collapse under her. She took the telegram and thanked the boy then walked to the seat at the end of the garden where she sat and placed the telegram on the seat beside her.

She stared at it, frightened to reveal its contents. When she did eventually pick it up and open it, her eyes were immediately drawn to the words *'KILLED IN ACTION'*.

Oh no, no, no, the tears came in floods and at that moment she felt she could collapse and die. *No, Sam! Not Sam, oh no, how can I exist without him?* Her mind ran wild. No picnics, no happy home-coming which she had been so looking forward to. *At least I won't have to tell him about Patch.* As if that mattered now.

Mary cried for the rest of that day and most of the night. She was numb with the realisation that her husband was buried somewhere in France and his dog in the wood. From time to time she washed her face and dried her eyes, but there were always reminders; fishing tackle, a cricket bag, photographs. A hollowness in her stomach ached for her husband and torrents of unhappiness would well up again and again. Then a feeling of anger. *He promised me faithfully he would definitely come home and all that talk about the simple life and picnics we were to have. How am I supposed to carry on without him?*

That night she took one of Sam's sweaters, rolled it up and used it as a pillow to feel something of her dead husband. She slept very little and in short naps, so that she gained sparse benefit from lying in bed. In the early hours the dawn chorus struck up and she found herself resenting the joy of the birdsong and wishing they would cease their singing. How could they be so happy on such a day with Sam not around to hear it?

She made a cup of tea and sat in the early morning sun on a seat outside the front door. She looked deep into the cup, trance-like, sipping gently as if she might find the answer to her grief.

Mary was at first oblivious to the young paper boy approaching. As he handed her the morning paper he noticed the swell of her breasts and, quickly, blushingly, averted his eyes.

He spoke, "Good morning Mrs Leftwich."

She looked up with a dulled expression on her face as if her eyes were not focused.

He spoke again. "Your paper, are you alright?"

She answered, "Yes I'm fine, thank you. I'm sorry, I believe your elder brother was killed in France wasn't he?"

The boy looked dismayed. He stuttered, "Yes, he was a hero, my mum and dad told me, and to be proud on him."

He stood in silence waiting for a response, his blue eyes expectant of a reaction.

After a few seconds which seemed like an age she said, "I've just heard my husband has been killed and someone has shot our dog, so no, I'm not really alright. Anyway, you'd better get on with your round. I was very sorry to hear about your brother."

The boy replied, "I'm very sorry but I don't know what to say."

He turned and slommacked away apologetically with his paper bag slung over his shoulder.

The news of Sam's death quickly spread through the village, the town and the county and cards of sympathy daily dropped onto the doormat in The Stables' hallway.

Chapter 22

When Laura Gittins got the news about Sam she went to her kitchen and wept. She got on hands and knees and scrubbed the red quarry tiles as a sort of penance and to take away the worries about Jabez and her feeling of anger. In a further attempt to banish these negative thoughts from her mind she set to baking a dozen scones. She sliced four of them and filled them with butter, jam and clotted cream.

Laura wrapped two of her scones and placed them in a cake tin, put them in the basket on the front of her old sit-up-and-beg bike and set off to visit Mary. It was a bright, warm day although there was no sunshine in Laura's heart as she pedalled past the village towards The Stables.

In the lane she stopped and spoke to Maurice Martin, who was weeding the edges around his front lawn.

"Good morning Mr Martin."

"Please call me Mosser."

"I'm going to see Mrs Leftwich at The Stables, she just lost her husband."

"Yes," he said, "I had heard, what a terrible loss."

"I'll push on," said Laura.

"Of course. Please give her my sympathy and tell her if she wants anything, I'm always around."

At the house, Laura leaned her bike against the open gate and walked down the drive, cake tin under her arm. She knocked at the door and there was no reply so she walked down the garden and called her friend's name.

A weak reply came, "I'm down the garden."

Laura found Mary sitting on the bench at the end of

the garden, looking out across the fields. Mary stood to face Laura and they embraced, holding each other as if they were sisters. Both women cried.

"I am so sorry," Laura's voice cracked, "I don't know what to say. It's horrible, he was such a lovely man, everyone loved him. Jabez is devastated and the village won't be the same without him."

Mary was unable to speak so Laura summoned up as much positivity as she could. "Let's go in and have a cup of tea. I've brought some scones with me."

In the large kitchen, Mary put the kettle on and Laura said, "You sit down, I'll do the tea."

The two women sat and talked about Sam's death. It affected both of them in different ways and Laura shared in Mary's grief while Mary recognised Laura's own worries about Jabez.

Chapter 23

In France the war rumbled on, Monty exchanging punches with Rommel. The Battle for Caen was a battle fought between the Allies, mostly comprised of British and Canadians, and German forces.

Caen remained the focal point for a series of battles throughout June, July and into August. The battle did not go as planned for the Allies, dragging on for two months because German forces devoted most of their reserves to holding the city, particularly their badly-needed armour reserves.

It took an exerted effort from the Allies and eventually, after two months of savage fighting and loss of life, Caen was taken and the whole of France was opened up for further advances.

To Jabez and Bert, however, it was their immediate surroundings and keeping alive which were their main concerns and the overall picture wasn't all that clear. All they could do was follow orders and put their trust in their officers and high command. They had both lost weight, through a combination of not enough food and the physical demands of warfare. Both also suffered battle fatigue and they, like many others, wanted the fighting to end so they could return to their homes.

Letters from Jabez arrived throughout the war and Laura related their contents to Mary. Consequently the two women became inseparable friends. There were snippets of good news from the various theatres of war in the newspapers, on the radio and at the cinema. One momentous piece of good news was the liberation of Paris and the surrender of the occupying German garrison on 25th August. This news sent a tidal wave of optimism across Britain that the final victory wasn't a million miles away and Germany would get its just rewards.

Newsreels recorded further successes. The thirteen-year-old gang, comprising Alan, Grinner, Clive, Stevo, Wacker and Terry were at the cinema on a drizzly Saturday night. They occupied almost a whole row. After complaints, the usherette came down the aisle and shone her torch on them, telling them to quieten down or they would be shown the door. The *Pathé News* featured the Battle of Paris and its fall and Terry started whistling, cheering and clapping. This set off the whole audience, who broke out into spontaneous clapping.

"Well done Terry," said Wacker.

When the feature film started, the lads all settled down to watch *Tarzan*; their favourite. It was their turn to ask some of the adults to be quiet as they were transported to the jungles of Hollywood.

On leaving The Gaumont, a spiteful rain bit their faces and they stood in the doorway of a shop which sold corsets and bras.

"Jane dunner need them," Terry observed.

"What great actors," Clive said. "Johnny Sheffield as Boy and that Maureen O'Sullivan's a bit of alright."

"I'd fight a tiger for her," said Terry with a lecherous grin.

Clive corrected him, "There are no tigers in Africa you prat."

"Well a croc or any bloody thing"

"I'd like to see that," Alan said.

"I like Cheetah the chimp best," said Grinner.

"That's because you look like him," said Terry.

"You're looking for a smack up the fizzog."

"You and who's army?"

The boys ambled off and peeled away to their various homes, their coats pulled over their heads against the rain. Gradually the group split up as they all went in different directions. Terry and Alan lived the closest together.

Terry started to run, shouting, "So long, see you tomorrow!" as he zig-zagged, dodging puddles.

Those years were full of incidents for the gang. They were a tight group and spent many of their waking hours together. Friendships were formed that were destined to stretch into adulthood and beyond.

One day, Terry had introduced a new member to the gang. He was an evacuee from London. He had a strange accent and when asked, "What's your handle?" he replied, "Bertie, Bertie All."

Now Bertie Hall was fired with enthusiasm and ideas; most of them impractical, some downright crazy. The boys had their own war, having running battles with the Back of the Sheds Gang. The rival gang came from the other side of the track, half a mile from the lads' stamping ground, on the other side of the brook down the disused railway line.

Bertie came up with a great idea. In the antique shop he had seen a Robin Hood-type hunting horn. "If we had the horn, one of us could hide in the water tower and if he saw the Back of the Sheds Gang he could blow the horn and warn us."

He took the others to the shop to show them the horn.

"But where are we going to find that much money?" asked Clive.

"Well," Bertie said, "if you all give me a shilling a month I'll hold onto 'em, and maybe we can take some beer bottles back to the pub and put that in the horn fund."

Terry chipped in, "I'll ask me dad for more pocket money, but he's as tight as a duck's arse in flight, so dunner hold your breath."

Religiously, they all contributed and the Horn Fund grew. In the meantime they kept going back to the shop to look at the horn. They amassed what to them was a small fortune. One more month and the horn would be in their hands.

On a bright Sunday morning, the lads went to call for Bertie to check the fund and make a payment, only to be told he had gone back to London. He had taken the fund and the horn stayed in the shop.

Clive said, "I knew we shouldn't have trusted him, he's a Cockney wideboy, inner 'e."

"Ar, they're all spivs down there, I wouldn't mind betting Bertie's dad were a spiv," agreed Terry.

It was altogether a bad experience for the lads, and secretly they felt pretty damned stupid. They put it to the back of their minds, committing it to history and chalking it up to experience. It was not until 30 years later, when enjoying a few pints in the King's Arms, that someone inadvertently mentioned Bertie Hall and the whole unfortunate episode was resurrected.

"That bugger took us for a ride," said Wacker.

"Yes, we were pretty stupid," Grinner agreed. "I wonder what he's doing now, probably got a stall on Petticoat Lane, just like Del Boy."

With an ear-to-ear grin Terry asked Alan, "How you getting on with Longlegs?"

At this point, Alan drained his pint. "Better go. And anything between me and Miss Longhurst is purely professional."

Jackie, from behind the bar, admonished Terry, "You always have to bring smut into it, Terry. Night, Alan."

Terry protested, "Well what's life without smut?"

After two years at their new house, the Taits had settled in and, as most of the work was completed they were able to enjoy the luxury of more leisure time. Alan was happy in his job and with the progress his children were making at the village school. There were three teachers to 35 children which was proving a very healthy ratio.

Alan repaired the bench at the far end of the garden; the very same one that Mary had sat on in 1944 when she opened the telegram telling her of Sam's death.

He replaced two of the struts which had rotted and painted the whole seat forest green, so it would last several more years. He used the seat when taking a rest from gardening and he couldn't shake the feeling when he sat there that he was sharing the space with someone else.

Spey loved to sit on the bench and would rest his head in Alan's lap. He was totally at peace and would drift off into doggy dreams, twitching and making muffled barks, chasing imaginary rabbits or diving into the brook. Alan found it fascinating that dogs dreamed just like humans. Even as he stroked Spey's head, the dog remained in his dreamland, oblivious to his surroundings and making muffled barks.

Man and dog spent many an hour in this peaceful way.

Chapter 24

In Europe, during the spring of 1945, the armies of the east and the west were engaged in heavy fighting in the race to take Berlin. As the enemy was pushed back, many of the German casualties were found to be children and old men. The soldiers of the Allies found the killing of children very traumatic.

In England, Mary was cutting her lawn, oblivious to what was happening across the channel; she had stopped listening to the news ever since Sam's death.

On the evening of 29th April 1945, Laura turned on her radio. It crackled into life and the news came in that German forces had surrendered in Italy. Although she knew Jabez was not in Italy, the news filled her with optimism as she felt the war would soon be at an end and the boys would be coming home. That night she poured herself a glass of sherry from a bottle which had remained unopened since the previous Christmas. She went out of the back door and raised her glass to the fading night sky.

"Here's to you Jabez, stay safe and please come home," she spoke out loud.

Thirteen days later, the news came that it was all over in Western Europe as on 7th May 1945, Germany surrendered to the Allies. Then, on 8th May on the Eastern Front, Germany surrendered to the Soviets. The whole of Britain breathed a sigh of relief and celebrations spread like wild fire with parties being organised in just about every street.

Laura picked up her morning paper and there it was in black and white – 'VE DAY', accompanied by a photograph of Churchill in Whitehall amid tumultuous crowds celebrating the end of the war. Happiness bubbled up in her. *Good old Winnie.* She had never felt such a volcano of emotion as she did at the thought that she would soon be reunited with Jabez and the tribulations of the last six years would be committed to history. A shroud of sadness enveloped her when she thought about Mary. No happy home-coming and no picnics for Sam.

Later that day she cycled up the lanes past the Cross Guns. The birds were nesting in the hedgerows and the hawthorn was in bloom, filling the air with the scent of spring. When she arrived at The Stables she knocked on the door but there was no reply.

She peered through the windows but there was no sign of Mary. Walking into the garden she shouted her friend's name.

"I'm down here."

Laura followed the sound to the end of the garden and there was Mary; a lonely figure sitting on her bench, staring out across her fields of dreams.

"Mary," Laura said, "have you heard the news? It's all over."

"Thank God!" her friend replied. "I'm so pleased for you. Jabez should be home soon."

Laura noticed Mary's eyes were moist and her lower lip had a slight tremble. She put her hand on top of hers, but did not know what to say.

"OK," Laura said after some thought, "we've got a party to organise and I need your help."

"Well I don't know."

Laura insisted, "You'll enjoy it. We'll hold it outside the Cross Guns. The whole village will pitch in, so there's no argument. It will do you good."

Mary, drying her eyes, said tentatively, "I can do some sausage rolls, but there won't be much meat in them. I'll add some bread and herbs, although there's

142

enough bread in the sausage meat already."

"That'll be fine, no one will know," said Laura.

"That Digger, he's a marvel though," said Mary, "he got me quite a few eggs so I'll make sandwiches too - egg and cress. Sam's favourite."

Chapter 25

Upon the defeat of Germany, celebrations erupted across the whole of the Western world. From Moscow to New York, people cheered. In London, crowds danced in Trafalgar Square, clambering over the lions and jumping in the fountains. Crowds lined the route of The Mall to Buckingham Palace, where King George VI and Queen Elizabeth, accompanied by Prime Minister Winston Churchill, appeared on the balcony. Flag-waving, cheering crowds massed in front of the gates and joy spread like a giant grin across the capital. Princess Elizabeth and her sister Princess Margaret were allowed to wander incognito among the crowds and enjoy the party atmosphere.

The village set the date for their own party on the Saturday following VE Day and the word went around quickly. The Women's Institute were in full swing on the cake front and the whole village was mobilised and in the mood to celebrate. Young boys were climbing trees, attaching banners from tree to tree across the street. There was a buzz of activity and enthusiasm. Union Jacks were everywhere, people brought tables out of every house and bedsheets for tablecloths from those that didn't possess one.

At The Stables on the Saturday morning, Mary was in the kitchen. She had dozens of sausage rolls on wire racks and was making up egg and cress sandwiches. She made them with love as if they were for her husband. She felt his presence at her shoulder and knew that, had he been there, he would be trying nick one before they got to the party.

To transport the food she had hit on the idea of using their old picnic hamper so she emptied it and lined it with clean tea cloths then carefully packed the sausage rolls and sandwiches in the wicker basket and buckled up the old leather straps. A wave of sadness came across her when she thought of Sam and how much he loved their picnics.

There was a loud knocking on the front door which startled her out of her reverie.

A young, fresh-faced Charlie Wilkins stood there with a broad grin spread across his face. "Laura Gittins sent me up," he said, "she thought you might need a lift and said could you bring a couple of chairs."

With the hamper laid on the back of Charlie's truck and two chairs half hanging out of the boot, they set off for the village pub. As they bumped off down the drive, Charlie, in an attempt at conversation, said, "'Ow you keeping then Missus?"

She quietly replied, "Oh I'm okay, you know. Okay, thank you."

The rest of the journey was conducted in virtual silence as Charlie didn't know how to make further conversation - only to say, "It's a lovely day for it."

When they arrived outside the Cross Guns the whole village was a blaze of red, white and blue and an air of happiness, activity and excitement prevailed from giggling girls to mischievous boys who ran about between adults in a frenzy of expectation.

All the tables had been joined together to form one long one that stretched from the front door of the Cross Guns right up the street, almost to the church. Charlie lifted out the two chairs and Mary took out the hamper.

"Thank you very much for the lift, Mr Wilkins."

"Please call me Charlie," he requested.

"Yes I will, Charlie, I will Mr Wilkins!" she replied.

The front door of the pub was open. Mary carried

145

the hamper inside and placed it on the nearest table. The front bar was packed with women buttering bread, making mountains of sandwiches.

The landlord, Jack Crosbie, who the villagers called Bing, was well into his 70s. He was a bald, portly man, fond of waistcoats of dubious design that only he would wear. He carried a fob watch on a chain in his waistcoat, which he always seemed to be winding up. He sported a thin moustache which was silver with brown tinges, the result of his habit of taking snuff.

"Everything going to plan, ladies? I'm opening the bar early today." He took another snort of snuff off the back of his hand and sneezed explosively twice into a large spotted handkerchief.

The food was taken out to the tables and covered in tea towels to keep the flies off the sandwiches and the wasps off the jam tarts. In the pub, men were downing pints and clinking glasses. Toasts were proposed to Churchill and all the men of the armed forces. The women busied themselves and the children stole jam tarts and chased each other round and under the tables. Two ATS women turned up and pitched in, preparing for the party by carrying extra chairs from the lounge inside the pub. Dogs of all shapes and sizes hoovered up any food that found its way onto the tarmac.

Mary sat down opposite a gaunt man, tall and thin with dark, sunken eyes and in a suit that hung off him.

"Morning," he greeted Mary, "are you a local?"

"Yes, I live just out of the village," she replied.

"I'm from the town, but my uncle lives here; you might know him - Jack Harris, had a butcher's shop in the High Street. I've just come back from Germany."

"Were you in the army?"

"Well sort of," he said, "I was captured at Dunkirk

and spent the rest of the war in a Stalag, so I didn't get to see much of the war. Although I did learn to darn socks, play the ukulele and speak the French language. Other than that it was a complete waste of time."

Mary thought to herself, *I wish Sam had been captured, maybe he would be with me now.*

"By the way, my name's Billy Harris."

"Pleased to meet you. I'm Mary Leftwich."

They shook hands formally.

"Would you like a drink?" he asked. "The bar's open."

"Well, er," she hesitated for a moment then said in a quiet voice, "thank you, that's very kind, I'll have a glass of white wine."

When Billy came back with the drinks they sat and talked. Both of them were glad to have company.

"Is your husband in the forces?" he enquired.

"He was, but he was killed after the D-Day landings."

"Oh I'm so sorry," Billy felt embarrassed and wished he'd never asked. He could see there was moisture building up in Mary's eyes, so he quickly changed the subject. "Lovely spread, when do we start eating it?"

As if by magic an army of WI members, along with Laura, started removing the tea towels and a large plump lady, Mrs Monica Wynstanley, barked out, "Help yourselves, everybody." She shouted at the children, "You lot go and wash you hands, we don't want your grubby little maulers all over the food, do we?"

Little Stevo Davies whispered under his breath, "Bossy old cow!" He tried to grab a rock bun but she retaliated with a quick slap around the ear. Stevo's mate Wacker used this distraction to nick a slice of Victoria sponge and he and Stevo - with stinging ear -

moved further down the giant table to try their luck elsewhere.

"Buggered if I'm washing my hands, I did that yesterday and they inner really dirty anyhow," Stevo said emphatically. "Here's Alan."

Alan appeared, sauntering up the road. Wacker greeted him, "'Ow do Alan, what you doing out?"

"I wanted to see what you country bumpkins get up to," Alan said jokingly.

"You hungry mon? There's loads of good grub here," Stevo told him, "but keep away from that big owd woman, she gave me a right smack up the ear, I could have punched her in the tits but 'er wunner have felt it."

After the party was over, chairs and tables went back into houses and sheets into wash tubs, but the bunting and flags stayed up for the expected homecomings of the forces.

Cheeky sparrows, chaffinches, jackdaws, crows and pigeons feasted on the crumbs of the celebration and the village slept in, only to be woken by the bells of St George's ringing for the Sunday service.

Chapter 26

Heads were buzzing as the faithful dragged themselves towards morning service. Irene Young, a stalwart of the church, looked down the village before entering and saw a uniformed figure quick-stepping it out towards her. As he came into focus she could see it was Ron Mitchell, home from the RAF. Ron was a tall, blond-headed, good-looking villager with a smile as broad as his shoulders. A navigator in the RAF, one of the Brylcreem Boys safe and sound after many sorties in Lancaster bombers over occupied Europe.

She greeted him enthusiastically, "Your parents have gone down to the church."

"Yes," he replied, "I called in at home and guessed that's where I'd find them, thanks Mrs Young."

Inside the church, apart from the light that came through the stained glass windows, it was dark and musty and it smelled of damp gravestones. Ron walked down the aisle and he could see his mum and dad next to each other, heads bowed, in the third pew from the front.

He sat down next to his mother. She turned to him and on sight of her son immediately burst into tears. They stood up and embraced, in front of the congregation. His mother was as round as she was tall and only reached Ron's chest. His dad looked close to tears too. Ron freed one hand and shook his father's.

"Welcome home lad," his dad croaked.

The rest of the service was a blur for the three of them, nothing registering. They simply wanted it to end as soon as possible so they could get home and catch up on the lost years. The vicar's sermon seemed endless.

When they left the church, blinking into the late morning sunshine, people patted Ron on the back. The vicar shook his hand, saying, "Well done my boy, thank God the Lord has spared you."

Ron thought to himself, *What about all the ones he didn't spare?* All those rear gunners that paid such a heavy price.

His mother smiled the same broad smile her son had inherited and his father was bursting with pride as the three of them linked arms and marched down the village to their home.

These sorts of reunions were daily happenings in villages, towns and cities across the nation as men came back to their families from Army, Navy and Air Force, victorious but damaged by their experiences.

For Mary Leftwich there was no such reunion and she faced up to the reality that although the war was over, for her the peace stretched out like a long, lonely road she would have to tread alone, without her beloved Sam. The hollow emptiness would be with her forever. It is said that time heals, but for Mary this did not ring true and she felt that part of her had died.

As the years rolled by the country enjoyed the peace and, although the war was not forgotten, the freedom and the end of rationing gradually came to be taken for granted.

Mary left The Stables in the year after Sam's death; it was too big for her on her own and heartbreaking to keep on living in the house which she and Sam had planned to fill with a family. She never got over the loss of her Sam and never looked at another man for the rest of her life.

Eventually, the Taits moved into Mary's old home

and it wasn't long before they felt as though they had always lived there. Alan and Donna's children grew up. Molly married and moved into town. She gave them a grandson called Jake who was a dead ringer for his grandad Alan. He always beamed with pride every time anyone remarked on this.

Spey died at the age of fourteen although he had still been a sprightly dog. Mysteriously, he became ill one weekend. The vet prescribed some pills as a potential cure but he did not improve and could hardly raise himself from his basket.

Alan said that if he was no better by the morning he would call the vet, but when Donna got up early and went to check Spey, he was already dead. She didn't need a vet to tell her that. She burst into tears and shouted for Alan, who rushed downstairs, fearing the worst. On seeing Spey he too burst into tears.

They buried Spey in a quiet corner of the garden, both sobbing as they dug the hole. They wrapped him in his blanket and buried him with his collar and lead and some of his toys.

When Alan told Bert and the lads in the pub the circumstances and how quickly he had died, Bert's explanation was that he had probably picked up one of Hooky's poisoned rabbits which he puts out to kill the buzzards.

Three weeks later Trotsky disappeared, and they found him dead in amongst the raspberry canes where he had gone to die.

The house felt empty without their animals and they needed time to adjust before thinking of another pet. In a strange way they felt it would be like being unfaithful to the dog which had given them years of enjoyment.

Jabez and Bert never forgot their friend Sam and

Laura Gittins ensured that she and her husband were never apart again for more than a day or two. Over time, Mary Leftwich became an extension of the Tait family and spent a lot of time at her former home with them.

Chapter 27

On 6th June 1994, Britain celebrated the 50th Anniversary of the D-Day landings. Jabez and Bert, both now in their 70s, were determined to go back to France. All across Britain there were parties, formal receptions and marches.

Across the channel more than one thousand paratroopers, including some veterans, re-enacted the mass D-Day Normandy drop which heralded the liberation of Nazi-occupied France. They descended out of a clear blue sky to launch the extensive French ceremonies.

A vintage Dakota dropped eighteen British and French senior officers over the village of Ranville, ahead of a spectacular display by nearly 1400 British, Canadian and Polish paratroopers who jumped at 800 feet from seventeen Hercules transports. After the display, members of the Allied countries marched. Some hobbled and some were pushed in wheelchairs by comrades past Prince Charles, who took the salute.

The main British events were at the Bayeux military cemetery and at Arromanches where the main seaborne British contingent had landed. Prior to the commencement of British ceremonies, hundreds of veterans, in berets and blazers covered with their decorations mingled with French visitors by Pegasus Bridge. Among that crowd of proud old soldiers stood Jabez Gittins and Bert Grimshaw, proudly displaying their medals. It all came back to them, the noises of war ringing in their ears; the fear, the mayhem. Not something they would ever want to repeat.

They both scanned the crowds, looking for familiar faces. Many wore sunglasses, others hobbled on sticks, some had lost hair and others had gained pounds. There were lots of wallets opened and photos that had browned with age were handed round.

Bert exclaimed, "Well bugger me, look who's over there!"

"Where?" asked Jabez.

Bert pushed through the crowds and got a closer look. "It is," he said, "it's owd Brummie."

With watery eyes, the two men gave each other a huge bear hug.

Jabez said, "It is, it's him, how are you mate?"

"Well I lost all me hair, but yow still recognised me."

Bert reassured him, "But yume still a handsome bugger."

"I'll never forget you giving me that bullshit about the Parson's nose, I always eats it but it never done me much good, although I do like the taste on it."

"Well baldness is a sign of virility, innit," joked Bert.

"Dow you be giving me that owd tosh."

"Okay, let's call a truce and see if we can conjure up a drink."

As they walked along the cobbled square, looking to quench their thirsts, people of all ages patted them on the back, thanking them and shaking hands. They felt such pride as they sat down outside a bar.

When the waiter arrived, Jabez took charge of the ordering, *"Bonjour, vous desirez trois bieres s'il vous plait."*

"Well bugger me, Jabez, I dinner know you could speak French!" said Bert with genuine amazement.

"I can only order me beer," he replied.

Bert took a gulp of his beer and asked, "What happened to that bird of yorn, her from Acocks Green you were always banging on about?"

"Oh 'er got married to a bloody Yankee airman, while I was doing me bit. Lives in Carolina now."

154

"See, if you had been getting the Parson's nose a bit earlier…"

"Leave off, Bert," Jabez interrupted.

They sat in the sun, drinking their beer, and opted for another round. Jabez raised his hand and the waiter came over. Jabez simply said. *"Encore! s'il vous plait."*

When the waiter returned with three foaming glasses, Bert exclaimed, "Well bugger me, yule a smart bugger and no mistake."

When the bill came Jabez noticed they had only put down one round. Jabez, being Jabez, pointed out the omission and the waiter said in English, "The first one was on the house," adding, "thank you for what you did for my country."

This sentiment was reiterated in a letter from Mr Mitterrand which was given to every veteran, including Bert, Jabez and Brummie, which simply read:

'To those who, 50 years later, have come to pay their respects at the graves of their fallen comrades, or to see again together the theatre of so much glory and so much suffering, I express the gratitude of France.'

The Queen and Prince Philip arrived by the royal yacht *Britannia* and altogether nineteen members of royalty, heads of state and government attended the D-Day celebrations, to round off what had been a truly memorable occasion.

The next morning the three men were driven, with other veterans, to the war cemeteries. They had a plan of the cemetery, supplied by the War Graves Commission, so it did not take long to find Sam Leftwich's grave. They stood, heads bowed, and only the ripple of a gentle wind broke the silence as Jabez, in a creaking voice started to read out the inscription *'RSM Sam Leftwich'*.

The voice cracked to a standstill, Jabez's shoulders hunched and he sobbed, "I canner do this," and turned away.

Bert also was reduced to tears as he put a sympathetic arm around Jabez's shoulder hoping it would convey his understanding. All three of them photographed Sam's grave, Jabez saying, "We've got to get a good 'un for Mary."

"Ar, she'd like that," agreed Bert.

The three red-eyed, tired old men, blowing into hankies, moved on along the rows of neat graves in the well-manicured cemetery, until they came to the final resting place of young Gareth Davies. Jabez explained to Brummie, "He was from our village, only 18, poor little bugger, never made it off the landing craft."

Bert also found the chaplain's grave, "God dinner do out for him did he?"

Disagreeing, the Brummie said, "But my owd mum used to say he works in mysterious ways, his wonders to perform, or summat like that."

"Well that's alright then inner it," replied Bert, "everything's hunky dory, but why Sam and why young Gareth? He were nowt but a kid."

Jabez asked the Brummie, "What is your real name? We canner keep calling you Brummie."

"I don't mind but it's Private Charlie Whelan."

They swapped addresses, promising to keep in touch, then Jabez said, "We'd better get our skates on, we dunner want to miss our bus."

"Dunner forget, Charlie, let us know if you're going to any regimental reunions or owt like that, we'll meet up and you can buy me a pint," said Bert.

Charlie Whelan walked off in the opposite direction. "Tara a bit, lads."

Bert shouted back, "Keep in touch, mon."

At the bus station there were many hugs and more pats on the back.

Several men shouted, *"Au revoir, merci and Vive la France!"*

In return there were cheers and the waving of Union Jacks, the Stars and Stripes, French, Canadian and Polish flags.

On the journey home the two reminisced about the weekend.

"I'm glad we visited the beach we landed on," Bert said.

"Yes, it was nice to see it calm, with the water blue rather than red. Although I could swear I felt the presence of the dead," Jabez said thoughtfully.

Bert enthused, "Weren't the French fantastic, what a reception! They seemed so grateful, especially as we flattened some of their beautiful cities."

Jabez said, "I think I'll come over again in the car next year and spend more time looking at all the other battlefields."

"We should bring Mary Leftwich," said Bert, "so she could see Sam's grave and how well it's looked after, I know she would like that."

As the ferry left Caen, they stood silently at the stern and looked back at the disappearing skyline of Normandy, the salt spray stinging their faces, remembering the trip 50 years before. It had been a totally different scene then, the channel full of ships belching smoke from their funnels as they approached France on a calm, moonlit sea on 6th June 1944.

As they disembarked at Portsmouth and boarded the bus to take them home, Jabez's enthusiasm to see his Laura grew ever stronger as if time had stood still and he was returning from the War. Although he had enjoyed the trip, just as he had been in 1945, he was glad to be on home soil. When he opened the gate to his smallholding, Laura came to greet him.

Even though Jabez and Laura had been married for over 50 years, the excitement was reciprocal. They embraced unashamedly, as two young lovers would do, their dogs vying for Jabez's attention, jumping at the fused couple.

When Bert was dropped off in the village he made a beeline for the Cross Guns. He turned to Doreen, "I may as well have a pint while I'm here Doreen."

"How did you get on in France then?"

Bert looked hard at the glass in front of him and drank half of it in one swallow, wiped his mouth, and said, "Perfect, fantastic, everyone was so friendly to us and we met some great people, although it was very emotional."

"Well you look a smart 'un Bert," Doreen observed.

"This 'ere's my demob suit - not bad, it only comes out for big occasions and it still fits me. I'm still at my best fighting weight. They gave us one when we was demobbed, out of one uniform into another as it were, made that Montague Burton a bloody fortune, you'd see the ex-soldiers looking for work at the end of the war, they all looked the bloody same."

Bert's ensemble was capped by his beret. Although it was faded with age, his cap badge as always gleamed with bullshine and his regimental tie was also in pristine condition.

Alan Tait came in through the side door as Bert was nearing the end of his pint.

"Fill that up again Doreen," said Alan, "and one for me."

Then, with pint in hand, Alan said, "Cheers and welcome home Bert, the place hasn't been the same without you."

"Ar, I know, I'm bloody unique I am," Bert replied, "has Digger been in?"

"No," said Doreen, "but it's a bit early for him."

"They were really good to us over there," said Bert, "so many kindnesses and a few free bevvies. Owd Jabez is pretty good at speaking Froggy an all."

Chapter 28

"**D**o you know anything about what's going on back of your house, Alan?" Doreen asked.

"No, why?"

"Well there's been some strange goings on down by them pools, from what I hear."

"How come?" he said. "I haven't been down there for a couple of days."

"Well there's been loads of panda cars around all day and the police have been asking questions around the village. Apparently, so rumour has it, they have found a body, we dunner even know who it is or whether it's a male or female."

"Funny, there's been no mention of it down at the paper. Perhaps I'd better get home and see what's going on. I'll let you know if I hear anything."

On his way home Alan called at Mosser's house, as he was the font of all local knowledge. The older man was in his garden when Alan pulled up and called out, "Evening Mosser, how's it going?" He got out of the car and leaned on the wicket gate, "Have you heard anything about the goings on behind my place?"

"Well I was up there earlier and they've taped off a whole area by the two pools. They've put up a white tent and some ribbon saying 'crime scene'. You're not allowed down there. And the police visited me, asking if I'd seen Willy Jones in the last 24 hours. Well, I told him, no not lately. Guess he's been up to no good again, bad lot that bugger."

Alan exclaimed, "Who the bloody hell is Willy Jones?"

"You know him, it's Hooky innit."

"Oh, I didn't know he had a name."

Mosser observed, "You're not alone, most people round here only know him as Hooky."

Back at The Stables, Alan went into the kitchen to find Donna. "Have you heard anything about the incident by the ponds?"

"No, but I know there's something going on. Nobody's been to see us yet."

"I think I'll take the dog for a walk and take a gander, see if I can see anything down there."

"But your tea's nearly ready."

"I won't be a minute," he replied, taking the lead and whistling loudly.

He crossed the two fields, keeping the dog on the lead. He went to the slightly higher ground but couldn't see anything discernible so turned for home.

After dinner he rang Chrissie Longhurst to let her know about the possible story.

"Thanks for that Alan, I'll look into it," she replied.

Emily Longhurst's niece Chrissie had followed her aunt's footsteps, working as a junior reporter on the local rag. She possessed the same good looks as Emily and the same gorgeous legs. Emily had married a farm supplies company representative and moved to Cumberland.

The next morning the cumulus clouds piled up like candy floss in the sky as Alan drove down Long Lane to meet Chrissie Longhurst.

She greeted him, "Morning Mr Tait, they've named the victim, an 82-year-local old man called Willy Jones, do you know him?" she said excitedly.

"Well sort of," he replied, "although we called him Hooky, I think he was a bit of a weirdo. He was very much the recluse; not sure exactly where he lived, but he always hung about around the two pools, he only had one hand, his other was a hook."

She squirmed, "Sounds a bit spooky."

161

"He was," Alan said, "No one liked him and I don't think anyone local will mourn him."

Emily said, "I'm going to see if I can speak to a policeman or maybe get some pictures at the crime scene, can you come with me? You know the area."

They walked across two fields. There wasn't much to see, however Alan took several shots of the tent using a zoom lens and more general shots of the location. On their return to where she had parked her car, a young uniformed policeman walked towards them.

Chrissie turned on her charm and with a coy look she enquired, "What's going on down there?"

"All I can tell you is it's a murder enquiry."

"Yes we gathered that," she said, "but I work for the local newspaper and I'd like to get something into the late edition."

He relented slightly at her pleading voice, "All I can tell you is the victim was shot and it must have been by a marksman as it was one shot right through his heart. If you want to know anything else, the Chief Inspector is due to make another statement tomorrow morning at headquarters. I'd love to tell you more, but it's more than my job's worth."

She said, "You've been most helpful, thank you. If you do learn any more my name is Chrissie and here is my card."

The policeman blushed slightly and carefully pocketed the card, like a prized possession. "I'm PC John Woods."

The next morning a gaggle of reporters with photographers were assembled at police headquarters.

"Chief Inspector Piggott," someone shouted out, "is he a local?"

The chief inspector looking somewhat annoyed.

"The victim is over 80 years old and we believe he is a local man…"

Another voice interrupted, "Do you suspect foul play?"

The chief inspector spoke again, "Yes, he was shot in the heart, we think from a distance."

"Any suspects?"

The policeman gruffly said, "Not at this stage, the body was discovered by two ramblers and, before you ask, we are not revealing their identities. That's all we are saying at this stage. Thank you."

The reporters were still calling for more information as the Chief Inspector left the room, shutting the door firmly behind him.

Chrissie Longhurst saw the young PC she had met the previous day, standing beside a door. She caught his eye and gave him one of her winning smiles. It induced another deep blush and he averted his eyes.

Chapter 29

The story in the local paper simply read, *'82-year-old Willy Jones mysteriously slain'* and one of the red-tops read, *'Puzzle at the two pools – 82-year-old disabled man murdered'*. The whole village was talking about it and the consensus of opinion was that whoever shot Hooky had done the village a favour.

When Alan got home that night he found that Molly, having heard the news about Hooky, had made a surprise visit.

"Dad," she said, "the other day when Hooky was killed I think I saw that soldier and his dog, call me daft if you like."

"Really?"

"Yes, he was right over there," she pointed. "I'm sure it was him and he was carrying something over his shoulder. Shall we tell the police, they're in the lounge with Mum?"

Alan replied, "No, no, not just yet."

In the lounge, Donna and two officers were seated, drinking cups of tea. Alan introduced himself.

"I'm Inspector Piggott," said the more senior officer, "and this is Sergeant Pat Hurst."

"I think I recognise you from the briefing this morning, I'm a photographer for the local paper," said Alan.

"Well," Inspector Piggott said, "As yours is the nearest house to the murder scene I thought it wise to ask if any of you had seen anything at all suspicious. Even the smallest detail can be important."

"No, nothing," said Alan emphatically.

The inspector asked, "Is there anyone you know around here that culls deer?"

"No," said Alan, "why?"

"Well, I'd like you to keep this to yourself for now. We have found a cartridge and a bullet which was imbedded in an oak tree - apparently it was from an old Lee Enfield 303. A rifle used in the Second World War. It has gone to Ballistics for further tests."

This sent waves of speculation through Alan's mind and for a moment he even considered that it could have been Sam Leftwich from the grave, avenging the death of Patch, but he quickly admonished himself. *Don't be ridiculous, a ghost couldn't... Anyway, I don't believe in the paranormal.*

There seemed no logical explanation, however.

The inspector said, "You looked a little startled when I mentioned the 303, any reason for that?"

"No, not at all," Alan stammered, "it just seemed a bit strange that anyone should have a 303 in their possession and I don't like the idea of someone wandering around with that sort of weapon, I was told it has a range of around 1000 metres."

Alan related the story of Owd Hooky firing his twelve-bore over his and Stevo's heads when they were kids. "I know that doesn't have anything to do with it," he said, "but it does sort of illustrate what kind of a man he was."

Sergeant Hurst said, "Do you know his pockets were stuffed with snares, shotgun cartridges, a catapult and ball bearings."

"Yes, that doesn't surprise me," Alan said, "he took pleasure in killing animals and birds, the wildlife around here certainly won't miss him. He liked to string them up in a row."

"How did he lose his hand?" Sergeant Hurst enquired.

"Well," Alan pondered, "I don't really know, although I heard it was something to do with farm machinery."

Inspector Piggott rose to his feet. "If anything else comes to mind please give us a call, and thanks for your help, it's been most useful."

The two officers drove off down the drive and Alan watched them go out of sight.

The investigation was ongoing; lines of officers did several fingertip searches, stretched out in a meticulous line, scanning the ground inch by inch. The only item found, aside from the 303 cartridge, was an old regimental cap badge which looked like it had been there for some time.

The police pursued several lines of investigation. Inspector Piggott made an appointment with Major Perriman at the local barracks. On his arrival at the guard room he noticed the floor had a high gloss shine and was surrounded by a pure white rope. This meant that if you wanted to speak to the duty sergeant you had to walk around the edge of the room, so that the floor would not be sullied.

Inspector Piggott explained that he had an appointment with Major Perriman.

"You must be the policeman," the duty sergeant bawled at the top of his voice. "I'll take you to him, Sar, follow me."

He then took off across the parade ground at a quick march, the inspector almost breaking into a trot to keep up with him.

On arrival at the officers' room, the sergeant knocked, opened the door and shouted, "The policeman is here, Sar."

This room was warm and inviting, with an open fire and a labrador dog prostrate on a rag mat in front of the fire. Inspector Piggott introduced himself and the Major rose to shake his hand.

"How can I help?" he asked in a soft, normal voice.

Inspector Piggott explained the enquiries they were making into Hooky's murder and the major responded by saying, "I have been following it in the local press, how are your enquiries progressing?"

"Not so well really," the inspector replied.

"So what can I do for you?" enquired the major; an erect man with a neat, clipped moustache.

"Have you ever had any rifles go missing? You see we found a cartridge from a Lee Enfield at the murder scene, but as yet no weapon has surfaced and I just wondered if…"

The major interrupted, "We no longer use Lee Enfield 303s in the army."

"Well it was a long shot, excuse the pun," the inspector replied, "but thanks for sparing me the time."

The major said, "You are very welcome and if anything comes to mind I'll contact you."

Eventually there was a breakthrough in the Hooky murder mystery. Two lads from the village found an old rifle. It was leaning against a tree in the thickest part of the wood which overlooked the twin pools. They carried the heavy gun towards their home amongst the village council houses, taking it in turns to carry it.

Bert greeted them, "What you got there, lads?"

"It's a gun, Mr Grimshaw."

Bert took it from them and had a look at it. There was no doubting it in his mind; what he had in his hands was a 303, the sort he had used during the war. He told the boys he was confiscating it and took it with him to the village phone box to ring the police.

The boys followed, shouting, "But we found it! Finders keepers, Mr Grimshaw!"

"Off you go lads, this is a dangerous weapon and

you could get yourselves into real trouble."

Following Bert's phone call, Inspector Piggott and Sergeant Hurst were soon walking up the path to Bert's cottage. He invited the officers in.

"This is it," he said, "the two boys found it in the woods by the twin pools where Hooky was shot."

He handed it to Inspector Piggott who inspected it carefully.

"It is a Lee Enfield 303. I know, I've used one," Bert said.

"Well done Mr Grimshaw, we will send it off to Ballistics."

Bert interrupted, "I can tell you for cert that that there is a Lee Enfield 303, no doubt about it."

The inspector smiled, "Yes! We simply want to find out whether the bullet we found was fired from this gun. Also we will probably ask the boys to show us exactly where they found it."

The report that came back from Ballistics stated that the bullet did match with the rifle but strangely the rifle was so old and in such a bad state that it was almost impossible to fire.

There was renewed interest from the media, running headlines like *'MURDER WEAPON FOUND'*, *'MURDER CASE REOPENED'* and *'WWII RIFLE MURDER WEAPON'*.

There was more police activity around the twin pools and more house-to-house questioning but again the wheels of justice gradually ground to a halt. Inspector Piggott retired from the force and Pat Hurst was promoted and moved to another area.

There were lots of theories around the murder of Hooky, but nothing concrete ever transpired. Day by day, interest diminished and the crime scene was disestablished, the pools being made open to the public once more.

Although for many, the WWII and 50th anniversary celebrations of D-Day were just a part of British history, for Mary it was a difficult time, as it was on a personal level very much in her consciousness. TV programmes and newsreels about the conflict opened up painful old wounds.

Laura was very aware of how her friend would be feeling and rang her to give her moral support as she also did every Remembrance Day.

"Donna has invited us up to The Stables this evening if you feel up to it," she said, "Jabez will drive us up there."

Mary hesitantly said in a quiet voice, "Okay, that would be lovely."

"Great. We'll pick you up around 6.30."

When they arrived at The Stables it was a still, quiet evening with thin cloud cover but warm enough to sit out. Molly walked across the lawn and greeted Mary, kissing her on the cheek, "Evening Mary, you look nice."

Swallows were performing low-level aerobatics with beaks full of insects and swifts screamed around, skimming over the house like demented fighter planes.

Mary asked Molly, "Where is Jake?"

"He's inside somewhere, mucking about with his toys."

Alan walked over with a beer in hand, "Like a bottle, Jabez? Want a glass?"

"No thanks, that'll do fine, saves the washing up."

Molly held Mary's hand, saying, "Shall we go down to our garden seat? I've got lots to tell you."

There was an affinity between Molly and Mary

which had grown since Molly was a little girl. The two of them would sit on the seat at the end of the garden, talking for hours on end. Donna was happy for the two of them; for Molly it was like having another granny and for Mary it was like having the child she was never blessed with. Donna had often wondered what they talked about for so long.

They often visited Patch's grave and Mary would watch smilingly as Molly tidied it up and placed wild flowers in an old jam jar on the dog's resting place. Mary thought, *I'm sure it was that Hooky that shot my Patch all those years ago, so maybe it was poetic justice, him getting a bit of his own medicine.* Walking back to the house, however, she felt ashamed of the way she had been thinking. After all, he was a human being and not everybody could be the same.

Molly held her hand, "Are you alright, Auntie Mary?"

She reassured her, "Yes, yes, I'm fine. I'm fine dear, fine."

At close of play on a Thursday evening, Chrissie Longhurst ran to Alan's car just as he was about to drive off from the newspaper. It was like a throwback and Alan pictured Emily striding across the car park to her Mini.

Chrissie leaned into the car, "Mr Tait, Emily told me about that photo you took years ago – the one with the man and the dog on it. Do you still have it?"

"Yes, what about it?"

"One of the nationals rang me to see if I could dig up anything on the Hooky murder. There could be a nice fee in it for me." She added as an afterthought, "And you, of course you as well."

Alan posed the question, "I can't see what my photograph has to do with the murder."

"Well it was rumoured that the image is of a soldier who was killed in the Second World War and what's more he lived in your house, yes and they say Willy Jones shot the soldier's dog."

"This is all very tenuous," he said, "you don't believe in ghosts do you?"

"No, not really," she replied, "but it is a bloody good story, and yes, yes also there's the fact that Hooky was shot with a World War Two rifle."

"I know, I know but we'll be laying ourselves open to ridicule or they'll say I doctored the photo, everybody does."

The slight flush on Chrissie's cheek persuaded Alan to reluctantly agree to give her a print of the photograph.

The following day he handed it over to her.

"Brilliant," she exclaimed, "I'll get it over to them, pronto."

She kissed him on both cheeks, continental style. Those soft perfumed kisses lingered and, although Alan had planned to cut the lawns that evening, he didn't much feel like doing that particular job.

He was always a sucker for feminine charms and young Chrissie had them in buckets.

Chapter 30

Alan was still enjoying the memory of those kisses as he approached the village and was quite pleased when rain speckled his windscreen and developed into a heavy shower, making it impossible to cut the lawn.

Instead he popped into the Cross Guns. Bert was at the bar and greeted him, "OK mon? Can I get you a pint while I'm here?"

"No, you're alright, I'm only staying for one."

Bert grinned, "Well I'm only getting you one."

Digger was of course in the window seat and as Alan and Bert joined him he asked, "Anything on the murder, Alan?"

"Do you mean since finding the gun? No, nothing new really."

Digger said, "It's a bloody mystery, I dunner think they'll ever find out who dun it. An old 303, who'd have one of them? Beats me. Mind you, whoever dun it, I say good luck to him."

Bert, wiping the froth from his mouth, argued, "But you canner go round shooting a body just cause they am a bit of a dirty bugger and a nuisance. They'd be bodies all over the bloody place."

Digger replied, "Well let's just say I wunner miss him."

Doreen shouted from behind the bar, "You'd better watch out what you're saying or you might find the coppers knocking on your door."

Alan drained the last of his beer, "I'd better get my skates on. Oh, it's still raining, good."

"Why good?" Digger asked.

"Well I promised to mow the lawn and I didn't fancy it," he said as he made for the door, "see you anon."

On Sunday morning Alan woke to a blustery day with spitting rain in the wind. After breakfast he picked up his three-year-old collie Poppy's lead, put on a light raincoat and set off towards the village.

The rain didn't amount to much and it was warm and humid with a good deal of insect life clouding the air as he walked into the quiet village. At the shop, Madge Simpkins greeted him, enthusing, "Have you seen the papers? Well this one in particular…"

She thrust a red-top towards him. The headline read, *'WHO KILLED HOOKY?'* alongside a picture of Hooky captioned, *'Heartless killing of disabled man in the heart of the country - see page 5'.*

Alan quickly turned the pages and there it was - his photograph with a red circle around the image of the soldier and dog, a full page. He read the first line, *'Local photographer Alan Tait captured this ghostly image.'*

"Bloody hell!" he said.

Madge pointed out, "There's more on the next page. They've really given it the full Monty."

On the next page there was a picture of The Stables.

Alan paid for his usual paper plus the red-top saying, "Thanks Madge."

Poppy sat outside patiently waiting for the off. On the walk home Alan kept glancing at the lurid headline and regretted giving Chrissie the photograph. The cloud started to break up and shafts of light burst through, exposing blue sky beyond.

Back at the house, Donna spread the pages out on the kitchen table, saying, "I'm not too keen on seeing our house associated with this tragedy."

Alan agreed, "Sorry love."

Donna complained further, "You know what'll

happen now, we'll get loads of newspaper men snooping around and morbid members of the public."

After breakfast Alan said, "It's dried up nicely so I think I'd better cut the lawn, while I have the chance."

Concern was written all over Donna's face as she said, "I hope Mary won't be too upset."

"I don't see why she should be."

Donna snapped, "Bloody hell Alan Tait, sometimes you can be so insensitive."

"Why, what have I done?"

"Well by implication, the paper is virtually accusing her dead husband of being a murderer."

"Well that's stupid," Alan complained and he went out to the garden, put petrol in the mower, primed it and gave the starter a long, sharp pull. The machine fired into action. As he cut the grass he thought of the ramifications of his photograph and he wasn't happy. He kept trying to justify it to himself but failed.

Lenin the cat, an offspring of Trotsky, was sitting on the bird table with his head sticking out beyond the roof. Alan stopped to empty the grass cuttings and spoke to him, "There's no harm in it, is there mate?"

The cat looked back at him impassively, as if to say, *'It's nothing to do with me.'*

Alan said, "Alright, it was a dumb thing to do, giving that photo to Chrissie."

Not many red-blooded men could turn her down though, he thought.

Alan went back into the house, saying triumphantly, "I've cut the grass, it looks much better."

"Good," Donna mumbled. "I'm bringing Mary over for a spot of afternoon tea."

Alan, looking to gain some brownie points, said, "I'll

sort out the table and chairs outside, it's brightening up nicely now."

There was little response from Donna, who didn't sport her usual smile as he tidied up and set out the table and chairs.

By early afternoon, as Donna returned with Mary, the sun was out and everything was rosy in the garden. At least Alan hoped so.

He went over to the car and offered his arm to help Mary out of the car.

"Ever the gentleman," she said smilingly.

"Have you seen the papers this morning?"

Mary answered, "Yes I have, you're referring to Hooky's murder."

"I am," he said apologetically. "I gave them that photo, but I didn't know it would be of such interest to them."

Mary shrugged her shoulders and said, "You know what these papers are like, make a mountain out of a molehill. But tell me, did you doctor that photograph?"

"No!" he said, "Definitely not, I swear it, cross my heart."

Mary sat down and fiddled with her pearl necklace. In hushed tones she said, "I'd love to see the original."

At this point Donna came out of the house with a large tray with a pot of tea, cups, milk, sugar and a plate of her home-made rock cakes.

"There we are," she said as she laid the tray on the table.

Mary said, "Sam would have liked this. He liked eating outdoors and loved going on picnics."

Poppy lay under the table, positioned so that if any food dropped she could quickly hoover it up.

Alan went off to fetch a print of the offending

photograph. He handed it to Mary who took out her spectacles and studied it, exclaiming, "That's Sam alright, and Patch, but it's a bit out of focus."

"You'll find this hard to believe, but Sam and the dog weren't on the negative."

She looked at the image again, puzzled and tearful, saying in a fading voice, "Sam always said he would come home. I'm glad he wasn't around when the dog was shot, Patch was his soulmate. It's a nice one of the house. Can I keep it?"

Alan said, "I'll do you a bigger print when I get to the office and I'll get it framed for you." He was trying to alleviate his feeling of guilt for putting the photograph into the public domain.

Photographers and reporters swamped the village and surrounds, following up Hooky's murder, looking for more angles to exploit and sensationalise.

Bert had told one of the reporters in no uncertain terms to sling their hook. He underlined it by saying, "You don't mess with me mate," as he pointed as his regimental cap badge.

Mary found herself the subject of attention, photographers peeping through hedges, knocking on her door and pointing cameras through her windows. She couldn't leave the house as they sat in cars waiting for her to appear. She thought to herself, *Now I know what these personalities have to put up with.*

One day when her doorbell rang she peeped through her net curtains and could see it was Donna. She unlocked the door, letting Donna in.

"Those vultures are still out there, I see," said Donna.

"Yes, I can't have a minute's peace, can't even put out the washing, they are always there."

Donna reassured her, "Well I've come to rescue

you. Pack a case and you can come and stay with us until the dust settles."

When they set off from the house, two cars followed. Donna pulled up outside the Cross Guns so as not to lead them straight to The Stables. The pressmen parked next to them, firing questions at the two women as they entered the pub. Mary and Donna did their best to ignore them.

Inside, Doreen greeted them. "Morning ladies, what's your pleasure?"

"Two coffees if that's okay," said Donna, "We're trying to get away from those reporters outside, they won't leave Mrs Leftwich alone."

As Doreen returned with the coffees, the door opened and the two newsmen stood at the bar. Doreen said, "What can I do for you?"

The taller of the two, a rat-faced man, ordered, "Two pints of what you sell most of."

Doreen drew herself up to her full 5'2" and said, "I can't serve you, you're banned."

The shorter, thick-set man, with a London accent, said, "Who banned us?"

Doreen replied with an obstinate grimace, "I did."

"When?"

"About 30 seconds ago," she said, "didn't you hear me?"

"What for?"

"Because we don't want you in the pub or the village," she insisted.

During the argument, Charlie Wilkins blustered in saying, "Have I got a thirst on me, pint of that Stowfield cider please, Doreen."

Doreen pulled his cider as she glared at the two men. They sidled out of the door, back to their cars on the car park.

Donna explained the recent goings on to Charlie. "They're going to hang about out there and I want to take Mary to our house, but I don't want those low-lifes to know where she's going."

"No problem ladies," downing the rest of his pint, Charlie said, "My car's on the back car park, I'll bring it up to the back door and you can sneak in."

Mary thanked him, "That's so kind of you, Mr Wilkins."

The two ladies got in the back seat. "Keep your heads down," Charlie said as he drove off.

As they passed the two cars he went at just the right speed so they could see what they thought was just the driver. When they arrived home, Alan said, "You've been ages."

"We've been locked in the pub," said Donna.

"Some of them press creeps are down there," said Charlie, "and they're probably still there, waiting outside for the ladies."

Alan thanked Charlie, "I owe you a pint."

"Well," he responded, "I'll drop you off, you pick up your car, you buy a me a pint, and bingo, job's a good 'un."

When the two of them parked at the pub, the press cars were still there with the occupants' eyes trained on the front door.

After some time, Rodent-features got out of the car, saying, "I'm bursting for a slash."

His mate suggested, "Why not? Ask if you can use the pub's toilet and you can see if the ladies look like leaving."

He went inside. As his eyes acclimatised to the dark interior he looked for a sign for the toilet.

Doreen came up from the cellar. "What do you want? You're banned."

"Yes I know," he said, "but can I use your toilet?"

"No you cannot!"

When he got back to the car, he said, "The bloody cow won't even let me use the bog, I'll have to go behind the bloody hedge. And the women aren't there anyway."

"They must be, I haven't taken my eyes off that door for a minute."

"Well they're not there, they must have gone out the back."

With that, after Rodent-features had relieved himself, both cars took off in the direction of the town.

Since the discovery of the 303, interest in the story had been resurrected. Theories of who carried out the Hooky murder continued to abound and suspicion was rife. Some thought it could have been an accident, but the fact that it was a clean shot to the heart and a 303 made that seem very unlikely.

To Molly Tait there was only one answer: he was shot by Sam as revenge from beyond the grave for shooting Patch all those years ago.

Donna and Billy discouraged her and only Alan didn't discount her explanation completely. Although he still told himself he didn't believe in the paranormal, ever since they had moved to The Stables he'd started to think again about what he did and didn't believe in.

Chapter 31

On a Sunday afternoon in October, Mary and Molly were sitting on the bench at the end of the garden. Poppy was flat out on the grass in front of the bench.

"Shall we go back in, Mary? It's getting a bit cold out," Molly suggested.

"I might just sit a while, if you don't mind. You go in though, I'm perfectly happy to sit here with my own company."

"Are you sure, Mary? Shall I get you another cup of tea to keep you warm?"

"That would be nice," said Mary.

The wind rustled the autumnal trees and as the pale sun cast long shadows, there was a chill in the air.

Molly returned with the tea and a shawl to put around Mary's shoulders before she headed back indoors.

Alan found Molly in the kitchen. "Where's Mary? I thought she was coming up today."

"She's on her bench. I've just taken her some tea."

Alan walked up the garden and found Mary still sitting silently with a peaceful, gentle smile on her face.

Poppy had gone indoors but Lenin the cat had moved from the bench onto the comfort of Mary's lap and was purring contentedly. Mary turned her head. "Alan, it's such a lovely evening, I just want to watch the sun go down."

"Fine," he said "shall I stay with you?"

The sun was a semi-circle of light quickly dropping behind the trees.

"Thank you," Mary said in a barely audible whisper, "That would be nice."

He moved the empty teacup onto the grass and sat next to her.

"I think Sam's coming home," Mary whispered, and she slumped sideways into Alan.

He, in panic, said, "Mary are you okay?"

Her breathing was faint, erratic, and, like the sun, fading.

The last bit of light fell behind the horizon and a dark, deathly shadow galloped across the landscape.

Alan felt for a pulse, but didn't have a clue about such things. Instead he cradled Mary in his arms as the cat looked on, as if concerned. Alan wasn't sure what to do so he opted to lie Mary on the bench and call Donna.

He ran into the kitchen saying, "It's Mary, I think she's dead, can you come?"

Donna, ran up the garden in a panic and on seeing Mary, said, "Oh my god, she has gone."

Molly, hearing the commotion from upstairs, followed on and burst into hysterical sobbing. "We'll have to get her into the house, we can't leave her out here in the cold."

Alan went into the house and returned with the carver chair from the dining room. He and Donna sat Mary in the chair and with one either side, carried her into the hallway. They both looked at each other.

"What do we do now?" asked Alan.

"I haven't a clue," said Donna, "I've never been in this situation before. Do we call the police or a funeral firm?"

They both agreed it would be best to ring Jabez, they felt sure he would know what to do. After receiving the call, Jabez and Laura drove straight to The Stables.

"Where is she?" asked Laura.

"We've put her in the lounge," said Donna.

Mary was still seated in the carver with the curtains

drawn. Jabez felt for a pulse, but it was obvious that she was dead.

Laura burst into tears, "Oh God, poor Mary."

Alan observed, "When I saw her first she had a distinct smile on her face. She whispered to me before she died. I think she said, 'Sam's coming home'."

Laura said, "We'd better ring Dr Westwood, he has to sign a death certificate doesn't he?"

Within the hour the doctor's pride and joy; a beautifully maintained Morris Traveller, pulled up at the front door of The Stables. Donna let Dr Westwood in and led him through to the lounge.

They all left the doctor in the room and went through to the kitchen. Donna put the kettle on.

Billy and Jake returned from their fishing trip and Billy asked, "What's going on Mum?"

"It's Mary, she has died," Donna ushered Jake out, asking him to go and play in the living room for a while.

Billy said, "Where's Molly? She'll be so upset."

His sister came into the room and brother and sister hugged, both crying; sharing their grief.

Molly told Billy, "I was only sitting with her half an hour ago. I can't believe she's gone, she can't have."

Dr Westwood eventually quietly emerged from the lounge, cleaning his glasses. In the kitchen he sat down, putting his bag on the floor. "As I suspected, it was her heart. I had been monitoring her heart condition for several years, it just gave up the ghost."

Molly was still crying and Donna wrapped her arms around her and cuddled her. Huge blobs of tears fell on her arm as she consoled her daughter.

Dr Westwood said, "You need to ring the funeral director now and they'll sort you out. Although I shouldn't recommend one," he added in hushed tones, "Portmans by the bridge in town is very good."

It was calm on the day of Mary's funeral; a haze dominated the morning, with the sun making a brave attempt to burn off the mist. She was to be buried in the village church, St Alkmund's. The whole village turned out for Mary, and Sam.

Alan and Donna walked down to the village with Molly, Billy and Jake following them down to the church. Outside, they met Bert, resplendent in his demob suit, with his faded beret and shiny cap badge. Digger was there too, almost unrecognisable in a charcoal suit that smelled of mothballs, a white shirt, a tie, and his wispy hair flattened to his head with Brylcreem.

Alan walked over to them and shook hands, saying, "Alright lads."

Bert for once was quiet and subdued as Mosser appeared. Donna stood back a little to let the men speak. However, she was soon surrounded by Madge Simpkins and a chatter of hatted ladies.

A sombre Jabez, with Laura on his arm, walked down the village and they joined the two groups. The sight of all those people assembled for his best mate's wife brought Sam's death back into clear focus and Jabez struggled to hold back great waves of emotion that made his throat ache.

He said, "I think we can go in now," in a shaky voice that revealed his feelings.

They all filed into the chilly church under the tolling bell. A musty dampness filled their senses, sparking off a bout of coughing which was amplified by the vastness and acoustics of the interior.

Mary's coffin was draped in the Union Jack and carried in by British Legion members. This was in recognition of the years Mary had spent in all weathers selling Poppies in the run up to Remembrance Day.

In the front pew, reserved for family, there were just three people; a man and woman with a girl who was presumably their teenage daughter. No one recognised them and whispers ran around the church, trying to identify them.

Alan and Donna sat in the pew behind Bert and Jabez and Alan looked at the backs of the two brave friends who had been through so much together. It sparked feelings of affection for his fishing mate and admiration of both of them.

The service went as most funerals do, with the vicar pontificating about a better life beyond and a place prepared for us. Alan thought, *I'd rather stay here*.

They sang *Abide with Me* then the vicar announced that there would be a reading by a member of the Leftwich family.

The teenage girl walked to the front and introduced herself. "I am Fiona Leftwich, great-niece of Mary and Sam."

She had the same aura of confidence that Sam always displayed, Jabez thought.

"This was a favourite poem of Great-Auntie Mary's, it's by Rupert Brooke."

She spoke loud and clear:

"*The Soldier*
If I should die, think only this of me:
That there's some corner of a foreign field
That is forever England. There shall be
In that rich earth a richer dust concealed;
A dust whom England bore, shaped, made aware,
Gave, once, her flowers to love, her ways to roam,
A body of England's, breathing English air,
Washed by the rivers, blest by the suns of home."

Fiona faltered at this point and hankies appeared all

over the church. Alan saw a river of tears running down Jabez's cheek and dripping off his chin. The old man was back momentarily in France; he imagined he could hear the gunfire, and he was holding Sam in his lap. Mary's departure was the end of an era and he thought of his own mortality. Laura squeezed his hand and passed him a hankie from her handbag.

Fiona continued bravely. Her voice cracked slightly as she read on,

"And think, this heart, all evil shed away,
A pulse in the eternal mind, no less
Gives somewhere back the thoughts by England given;
Her sights and sounds; dreams happy as her day;
And laughter, learnt of friends; and gentleness,
In hearts at peace, under an English heaven."

A red-eyed, chattering congregation left the church, shaking hands with the vicar and thanking him. "Lovely service, Vicar." Some of them meaning it, others merely being polite.

Once clear of the church a lot of them lit up cigarettes and they all headed towards the pub.

Bert said, "That girl read the poem beautiful, the rest on it were a load of mumbo jumbo. I'm nipping home for a minute. See you in a jiff."

Madge Simpkins and Doreen had laid out a huge buffet on trestle tables right down one wall of the bar. Red-faced Charlie Wilkins had positioned himself near to the buffet, waiting for the time when the food would be served. Nicker Stevens had side-stepped the church bit, but didn't want to miss out on the free grub and had put on a black tie. He too was standing near the food with a pint in his hand.

Jabez made a point of going over to Fiona and

congratulating her on her reading of the poem. He introduced himself to the three Leftwich family members, "I'm Jabez, Sam was my best mate."

The man introduced himself, "My name's Brian and this is my wife Maureen - and my daughter Fiona. Sam was my uncle."

The vicar, Rupert Wilkinson, was on his third slice of quiche and his third pint of Shires when his wife said, "I think we had better think about going, my dear."

People gradually left and eventually there was just the Leftwiches, Mosser, Digger, the Taits, the Gittins, Bert, and Charlie Wilkins - who was still piling up his plate from the buffet.

Brian Leftwich announced, "I'd like to buy you all a drink."

Jabez said, "That's not necessary, mate."

Bert, however, never one to miss an opportunity, smiled and said, "That would be nice."

Brian said, "Well you've all been so kind and I know Auntie Mary would have liked that."

They all raised their glasses as Brian gave a toast to Auntie Mary and Uncle Sam.

Bert and Jabez rarely talked about the war. It was too painful an experience and the real horror of it wasn't something to be dwelling on. However, on this occasion they did relate the details of Sam's death and what a loss he was as a leader, soldier, sportsman and most of all as a friend.

"He was the best cricketer for miles around and he taught me to fly fish," Jabez said, "He was one of those people who could turn his hand to anything."

"I think Sam was very lucky to have friends like you," said Fiona.

"And we were lucky to have known Sam, he was irreplaceable and my very best friend."

That night, Jabez was plagued with vivid nightmares of Sam and Normandy, mixed up images; Caen collapsing in dust, explosions, gunfire and death all around. He saw Sam walking on a hill and Hooky by a pool. He saw Sam take aim and Hooky fall grimacing and ashen-faced. He woke in a cold sweat, shouting, "Sam!"

Laura woke, "What is it darling?"

"Just a dream," he said, "just a dream."

The day after the funeral, Molly walked down her parents' garden. She wanted to be near Mary. A heavy dew soon soaked her sandals. She sat on the bench she had shared so many times with her friend. Poppy followed on and jumped onto the bench, resting wet paws and her chin on Molly's skirt. It was as if she sensed her grief and wanted to comfort her.

Molly looked up towards the skyline where she thought she could see a man with his arm around a young woman. Running beside them was a small barking dog. Poppy cocked her ears and put her head to one side. The couple disappeared out of sight over the horizon and Molly felt happier.

When she walked into the kitchen, Molly said, "I'm sure Mary and Sam are together now." She whispered to her father, "I've seen them."

He did not contradict her.

Gradually, as time passed, the Hooky murder faded, drifting slowly into the past to become a part of local folklore; an unsolved mystery, a closed police file and almost a legend.

Following the story around Alan's photograph, Chrissie Longhurst took her long legs to London. Because of her contribution to the story, she had acquired a well-paid job with the national red-top which had originally featured Alan's photograph.

The only concrete reminders of Sam and Mary were Mary's and Patch's graves and the memorial bench at the cricket club.

However, Alan always felt their presence in his home and he felt comfortable with that.

Molly remained convinced the vision she had seen was not a figment of her imagination. She knew that Mary, Sam and Patch were by a brook somewhere, enjoying a picnic.

Printed in Great Britain
by Amazon

67990252R00116